# Hostile
# INTENT

## BLACK TOWER SECURITY

# TARA GRACE
# ERICSON

Edited by BH Writing Services & Editing Done Write
Cover Design: Jess Mastorakos

Paperback ISBN-13: 978-1-949896-42-8
Ebook ISBN-13: 978-1-949896-41-1

*To those fighting impossible battles.*
*We know who wins the war in the end.*

"Thus says the Lord to you, 'Do not be afraid and do not be dismayed at this great hoard, for the battle is not yours but God's.'"

2 Chronicles 20:15a

# CONTENTS

# CHAPTER ONE

COLE KENSINGTON SIGNED the check and slipped the black card back in his wallet. He looked back up at his long-time friend. A friend who also happened to be the owner of a private security firm-for-hire that he'd made use of several times before.

"I've known you for a long time, Flint. You know I appreciate everything you and Black Tower have done for me. But this one…it's tricky."

That was the understatement of the century. The truth was that literally everything Cole had worked on for his entire life was on the line. And if Flint couldn't help? Well, then Cole didn't know what he'd do.

Flint nodded from his seat across the small table of the cozy lounge, tucked inside an old building, steps from the brick-lined sidewalks of King Street in Old Town Alexandria. "I understand. You've got to protect your company."

Cole nodded, but it was more than that. Zia Pharmaceuticals was more than just a company to him. They changed peoples' lives. He'd spent his entire life with the solitary goal of advancing Alzheimer's treatment and prevention. He might not be in the lab as a researcher anymore, but the work his company did was still why he showed up every day. And why he'd been adamantly opposed anytime the board of directors hinted toward an acquisition.

But there was something going on, and he needed to get to the bottom of it. Which was where Black Tower Security came in. Flint's elite team of private security agents was the best in the business. He'd hired them for everything from training his in-house security team to using them for additional security for an important transport of bio-hazard samples.

He rubbed the rim of his glass with his finger. A casual movement, but one that gave his restless hands something to do while they talked. "So, you've got a plan?"

Flint looked briefly across the room, then met Cole's eyes again. "I've got the perfect person. If you can get Joey plugged in as some systems analyst or security specialist…" He waved a hand. "Basically anything around your computers and you'll be set."

Cole leaned forward, eager to hear more of the plan. "That's easy enough. We've got an opening in Internal Tech right now, actually. And you're sure Joey is the right one for the job?" He wanted to trust Flint on this. He *did* trust the man, but this was his everything. "I'm not messing around here. I *have* to find the mole. There's no other option." His chest tightened painfully as the weight of the problem pressed in around him.

Flint bent his head slightly forward. "I'm telling you, Joey is the one you want. If there is something hidden in your systems or someone stealing information, Joey will find it…or them."

Cole let out a huge breath at Flint's firm endorsement. Knowing that someone Flint trusted would be on the job was incredibly reassuring. "Good. I'll want personal updates about what he finds."

Flint smirked, and Cole heard a small laugh.

He tipped his head in confusion. "What? Is that a problem?"

"No. It's just that… You should know…Joey's a woman." Flint leaned back in his chair and crossed his arms over his chest.

Cole mentally rearranged the assumptions he'd

already made. He couldn't tell if Flint's posture was preparing to defend his employee or simply trying to get comfortable.

Before he could respond, Flint continued. "She's the best hacker I've ever seen. She worked for me at Raven Tech…and well, let's just say before that she was wearing a different color hat." Flint's stern, protective tone suggested that Cole would be better off not asking questions about her past.

Cole raised his eyebrows in surprise at the admission. "But you trust her?"

Flint bowed his head slightly. "With my life. And the lives of every single one of my men."

That was quite a statement. Cole knew just how much Flint invested personally in every operative at Black Tower. He lifted his hands and spread them in invitation. "Well, all right then. When can I meet her?" He needed to size this woman up for himself. Especially since he was apparently going to let her inside the fortified walls of Zia's computer network.

Flint glanced across the room and signaled someone with a head nod. She was here? Cole followed the motion and searched the room for the infamous Joey.

When he realized the woman walking toward

them was actually walking *toward them,* his mouth went dry.

Initially, he expected to create a cover for a pale-skinned, balding guy with a soft belly who would fade into the woodwork of the IT department. When Flint had said Joey was a woman, Cole realized he'd simply switched the gender of his imaginary person. It hadn't prepared him for the gorgeous woman in front of him. Even without the red dress she wore tonight, she would never fade into the woodwork. Anywhere. This was the woman who could program circles around the team at Raven Tech?

Flint stood as she approached, and Cole scrambled to do the same. "Cole Kensington, may I introduce Josephina Rodriguez?"

He caught the friendly eyeroll she flashed her boss before she turned to meet him. "It's Joey," she corrected firmly.

Her dark-brown eyes met his with a spark of irritation. All traces of the humor she'd shown to Flint were gone. He held out his hand, thankful for the decades of business meetings that helped his body complete the expected greeting automatically, since his brain was currently short-circuiting at her arrival. "Pleasure to meet you, Joey."

Cole was pretty good at reading people, and by his estimation, Flint's ace programmer was definitely not pleased to meet him. But why? He'd never done anything to her, as far as he knew. Maybe they'd interrupted something. A date perhaps. That would explain the striking red dress that currently had every eye in the place glued to her. It wasn't exactly standard for a business meeting, and it made her impossible to ignore. Flint thought she should go undercover? The woman would stick out like an intern at a board meeting among the staff in his ITS department.

If he decided to let her in at all.

———

Joey considered a moment before taking his offered hand. She'd seen his photo a dozen times as she looked through news articles and his Wikipedia entry. He was taller in person.

And more handsome.

Her research had revealed how he'd worked his way up in the company from researcher to technical director and taken over the reins from the previous owner and CEO. Now, he owned a 30% stake in the company that was on the forefront of cancer and Alzheimer's research.

Rich, smart, and good-looking?

Why was the world so unfair?

At least she had the skills to help correct the imbalance. Flint hadn't mentioned why he wanted her at the meeting, but the CEO of the pharmaceutical giant was high on her list for suspected ties to the Syndicate.

It was impossible to operate in the criminal world without hearing about the mysterious Syndicate, an ultra-secret circle of corrupt elites who seemingly had their fingers in everything from drugs to weapons and human trafficking. But after she and Ryder had discovered that the Syndicate had been responsible for trying to kill Flint's sister, Fiona, it became personal. It became her mission to take them down.

She and Ryder were just starting to unwind the web of the Syndicate and all the players. Digging through potential baddies, it seemed like every big-name corporate head was interconnected, along with every politician.

The list of potential members of the Syndicate was basically a list of who's who in America. And Cole Kensington was always sure to be included on that list. But he was a good friend of Flint's. If it turned out he was also Syndicate? Well, there would be an entire team of muscled ex-SWAT and military guys to take care of him.

No doubt Ryder would be first in line.

She hadn't crossed Cole off her Syndicate suspect list, despite Flint's intense dismay when she'd brought her suspicions up once before. She disagreed with her boss, but she wouldn't say anything more until she had proof. Kensington may have pulled the wool over Flint Raven's eyes, but he wasn't fooling her. No one came to be as successful, rich, and powerful as he did without a few skeletons in the closet. Plus, Zia was raking in billions of dollars charging for medications they'd *altruistically* developed to help people—something that always made her blood boil after what happened to her sister.

Everyone in the dark web circles she still haunted knew to let her, aka Phoenix, know if they heard something about Kensington. The chatter in one of her vigilante hacker chatrooms was that Kensington was looking to acquire Placana—the same company she blamed for her sister's death. The deal would likely bring him billions in additional revenue, as if Kensington wasn't rich enough already.

Joey knew he had more than a few ties to the nefarious band of powerful elites who had targeted Flint's sister and Ryder's fiancée, Fiona. Which was why it was all the more frustrating that Flint didn't see the obvious facts. Cole Kensington was part of the Syndicate; he had to be.

Instead, Flint treated him like a friend, and Zia was one of Black Tower Security's biggest non-government clients. At least for now, Black Tower would be safe from the Syndicate. She'd make sure of it from her favorite spot–right behind her computer, where she kept an eye and an ear on everything. Just how she liked it.

"Nice to meet you, Mr. Kensington." Quickly dismissing him, she turned back to Flint. "Are you going to tell me what's going on? No, wait. Let me guess." She looked the surprisingly muscular CEO from head to toe. Everything she knew about the man made her dislike him. "Mr. Kensington needs the paper trail of a secret baby to disappear?"

His expression darkened, and he began to shake his head. She continued, her imagination running wild with accusations she was sure he deserved. "Do I need to erase his presence from a flight? Adjust his previous tax returns? Get the city to lose his parking tickets?"

Her fingers twitched in irritation, so she leaned them on the chair in front of her. Flint wanted her to help this man, and the thought made her crazy.

Cole's expression turned to one of laughter, then he paused. "You can do that?"

She shrugged. "Which one? The IRS? Easy. Delta Airlines? Slightly harder, but yeah. I can do that. So, what is it, Raven?" She'd like to get this over with and get back to her desk. That was where she could protect her team. Being out here was a waste of her time, especially if Flint wanted her to help this man. She trusted Flint without question, and they'd taken work from Cole Kensington before, but their friendship had always made Joey a little uneasy. The more Joey had dug into various confirmed and suspected Syndicate members, the more she was sure that Kensington was involved. There were too many threads tying back to him.

Even if she'd rather be anywhere else, here she was.

Because Flint asked her to be.

Her hands went to her hips. "This seems like it could have been an e-mail, Flint." She referenced his favorite mug, emblazoned with the saying. He hated unnecessary time wasted in meetings. Which made this meeting all the more suspicious.

"I wanted to do this in person," came his response. Flint gestured for them all to sit down, but

Joey only raised her eyebrows. She wanted more information before she was willing to play along.

He sighed in response and took his seat. Cole waited a brief moment, watching her, then sat down as well.

Flint's hand came to his face and rubbed his jaw before looking up to meet her gaze. "I won't pull any punches, Joey. You've got a new assignment. Starting Monday, you'll be undercover as a full-time employee at Zia Pharmaceuticals."

She went completely still, her muscles frozen as she gaped at her boss. He had to be kidding. This was some sort of joke he was playing, right? She gripped the back of the chair tightly, as though holding it would help hold her together.

She blinked long and slow, considering briefly if when she opened her eyes, she'd be back in a meeting at Black Tower Security. Perhaps she fell asleep during a debrief. It had been a long week.

But when she opened them, the scene in front of her remained unchanged. She looked back and forth between the two men. Flint seemed confident and slightly amused at her reaction, flipping his gaze between her and Cole. She narrowed her eyes and considered changing the default keyboard layout on his computer so it would type gibberish.

Cole, on the other hand, had his eyes zeroed in on her. His brow was furrowed, his mouth tugged to one side.

Hesitantly, she pulled the chair out and took a seat at the table with two of the richest men in Alexandria.

The first, she trusted with her life.

The other was most certainly a part of the organization that had kidnapped Flint's wife and blackmailed his sister. And apparently, he was her new boss.

# CHAPTER TWO

JOSEPHINA RODRIGUEZ TUCKED in her blouse and glowered at the reflection in the mirror. Undercover at an office building? Her boss had definitely lost it on this one. He'd interrupted her girls' night out so she could attend the meeting at Hamilton's, then ambushed her with the fact that she would be working for Cole Kensington. She was definitely messing with his keyboard.

"What was Flint thinking? I can't do this," she moaned, turning toward the phone propped on the dresser.

Miranda Bradley's laugh came quietly through the speaker. The screen only showed an empty kitchen, but as Joey grabbed the phone, her friend appeared from off-camera.

"Oh, sweetie. Yes, you can. Anyone else, I'd agree. But Flint wouldn't send you in if he didn't think you could do it."

She flashed Miranda a skeptical look. "I'm not so sure about that." Unfortunately, Miranda only knew half of the story. The only other member of Black Tower that knew she suspected Cole Kensington was Ryder. The two of them had been digging into the Syndicate for months. And now she had an opportunity to go inside the lion's den and suss out for herself just how deep Kensington's involvement went.

She'd do whatever it took to protect Flint and her team at Black Tower. When she finally had some real dirt on Cole Kensington, it might be hard for Flint to accept, but she couldn't be worried about his feelings.

"How do I look?" She stepped back from the phone so Miranda could see the full ensemble.

She was wearing an awful, shapeless button-down shirt and a pencil skirt she normally wouldn't be caught dead in. Inside Black Tower Security, where she usually sat in her own war room of computers, she was far more likely to be in sweats and a tank top, with her curly hair loosely bound in a scrunchie.

Not at Zia Pharmaceuticals, though. There was a dress code, Mr. Kensington had ever-so-kindly informed her. Thoughts of the successful pharmaceutical CEO made her usual morning scowl somehow scowlier.

"Oh, my." Miranda's reply told her everything she already knew. "At least your hair looks good?" she offered with an optimistic lilt.

Joey glanced at the clock near her bed. It was six-thirty. She was supposed to report at seven, which meant she needed to leave soon. With a sigh, she ran a hand over her hair, missing the feel of her normal curls. She'd straightened her hair last night and it hung over her shoulders. Cole hadn't specifically mentioned her hair in his dress code comments, but she'd seen his eyes flicker to it when he said the words. Cue all the teenage insecurity she still carried about her unruly hair.

The buzzer sounded. She frowned. "Someone's at my door. We'll talk later, okay?"

"No worries. I've got to jump in the shower anyway. I want to hear everything later tonight, though!"

Joey waved good-bye and disconnected the call just before she hit the intercom button.

"What?" Her tone came out a little harsh, but she wasn't in the mood to be friendly to a visitor who showed up before seven.

"Good morning, Miss Rodriguez. Mr. Kensington

is waiting for you in the car."

She narrowed her eyes and jogged to the window to take a look. A sleek, black town car was parked in front of her building. The windows were tinted, but was that a shadow in the back seat? She hurried back to the intercom. She wanted to argue and suggest exactly what Mr. Kensington could do with his early-morning surprise visit. But it wasn't the arrogant CEO at the door. It was his driver. Because, of course, he had a driver. Probably wearing one of those little hats. And she'd feel bad yelling at the messenger.

"I'll be down soon," she said. She'd take the ride, but she wasn't going to hurry on Mr. Kensington's account. This little visit hadn't been in the agreement. And she didn't run when just anyone called.

Flint? Him she would come running for. He'd been her boss at Raven Tech after she landed in a heap of trouble. He'd managed to get the charges dropped and gain her eternal loyalty at the same time. She was the one he called when Jessica was kidnapped, and now she worked for him at Black Tower Security.

It was the members of BTS who comprised the remaining list of those she would come running for. Ryder, Tank, Marshall, and Jackson. And, of course, Miranda. They were the closest thing Joey had to family, and she'd do anything for them. More than once, that meant answering her phone at three in the morning or dropping everything in the middle of a trip to the gym.

But Cole Kensington? He could cool his designer Oxford heels while she finished getting ready.

If only she wasn't already done. She glanced at the coffeemaker, considering whether she could make him wait the eight minutes it would take for the machine to make a pot of disappointing drip coffee.

That was probably pushing it. Instead, she went back to the bathroom and fussed with her hair, taming the flyaways at her scalp and applying just a touch more eyeliner. As if makeup was a shield, and she was going into battle. Which she was. Flint may have sent her to protect Cole Kensington and Zia Pharmaceuticals from some invisible threat, but she was admittedly skeptical that such a threat even existed. Her own mission was far more delicate. And she needed to be on top of her game to investigate Kensington while right under his nose.

Finally, when there were no other tiny tasks to delay her, Joey grabbed her turquoise leather backpack and headed downstairs.

It was time to face the target. Handsome and charming as he might be, that's what her new fake boss was. Cole Kensington was a suspected hostile operative, and she was going to dig until every last one of his secrets was revealed.

---

Cole flipped through emails on his phone and shifted restlessly in his seat. His irritation flared at having to wait for Miss Rodriguez. Wasn't she supposed to be the best? He'd told her to be at the office at seven, so she should have been nearly ready to leave when he arrived.

Initially, he'd planned to meet her at the office, but after further consideration, he decided it was better for them to meet beforehand, so her first day would appear completely normal to anyone whose interest was piqued by her arrival at Zia.

If she was going to be effective at solving the mystery within his company, no one could suspect that Miss Rodriguez was anything more than she claimed—a newly hired member of the Internal Technology Security team. ITS was Zia's own little Department of Homeland Security. Their sole mission was to protect Zia from enemies–foreign and domestic. But it seemed to him they weren't quite doing their job.

He checked the time on the top of the screen again. "Did she say how long she would be?" he asked Jared, his driver and personal bodyguard.

"No, sir. Just that she would be down soon."

Cole chewed the inside of his cheek to disguise his frustration. He forwarded an email to his Director of HR. Another went to his Director of Research.

The door to his right opened and a blast of chilly air filled the backseat as Joey climbed in. Jared closed the door behind her. Even though he'd been expecting her, he immediately felt flustered at her presence. The space filled with coconut and citrus as the hot air from the vents once again surrounded them both. The awareness of her nearness caught him off guard and heat climbed up his neck. The tropical aroma made Cole want a tropical drink and a seat with his toes in the sand.

As though he'd taken a vacation in the last five years. While he knew other CEOs in his business often booked "work meetings" at fancy resorts, Cole had been laser focused on business. He was tired. Lord knew he could use a vacation.

He shook his head to clear the ridiculous notion. Someday, he'd rest. But not today. Probably not even this year. There was too much at stake.

"Nice of you to join me," he said. Then he immediately regretted the snarkiness in his voice. He'd been told by more than one friend that he needed to control his tongue. Even when things were stressful, it was no excuse to treat people poorly.

Miss Rodriguez raised an eyebrow at him. "Good morning, sir. I certainly apologize for making you wait. I wasn't expecting a personal visit so early."

He could hear the insincerity of her apology in the saccharine sweetness of her words. He forced his face into a smile. "It's no problem at all. My fault for arriving without notice." Unlocking his phone, he held it out to her. "Put your number in, so I can contact you directly in the future."

He saw her cheek twitch, but she did as he asked. When he held out his hand to her after she finished, she hesitated. Perhaps she was second-guessing his having her number?

"It's purely business," he said to reassure her. "I'm not interested in anything more."

She chuckled. "That makes two of us, big shot. Here." She tossed his phone in his lap instead of placing it in his hand and it dropped to the floor. "It's in there as Joey."

He fished the device from the floorboard and swallowed his disappointment at her quick dismissal of him. He didn't want her to be interested. It would only complicate things. So why did it sting that she wasn't? He rolled his shoulder to shrug off the odd feeling. Maybe he was just too used to being fawned over by shallow women trying to impress him. He'd just barely met her, but he already knew without a doubt that Joey was neither.

"Good. Glad we're on the same page," he confirmed. Better for both of them that it was clear from the beginning. Even if he hadn't truly stopped thinking about her since dinner. "Now, let's talk business. You saw the material I sent on Saturday?"

Joey nodded. "I got it Sunday morning."

He vaguely remembered looking at the clock after he sent them. Nearly midnight. What did it say about him that he was working late into the night on a Saturday? What did she think? He bit his cheek. It didn't matter what she thought.

"I've touched base with Human Resources and you are all set to do the standard week of new-hire orientation. As far as anyone else at Zia is concerned, you are a new employee in the ITS department. The job opening was posted several weeks ago, so no one should be surprised, other than we don't usually fill a position quite so quickly. We'll meet outside of work hours. If you have something urgent to discuss, you can send a message to this number"—he handed her a card—"and I'll find an excuse to summon you to my office."

"Who is my supervisor?"

"Me," Cole responded automatically. "No one else at Zia knows about you."

"I meant for my cover. Who is my fake boss? Who could fire me and ruin everything?"

He felt heat rise under his collar, embarrassment at his quick assumption. "Oh. You'll report to the Director of ITS. His name is Patrick Wragge. He's been with me for ten years or so and I trust him. But he's still not in the loop on this. He thinks you got the job as a favor to a family friend," he added with a hand wave.

Joey groaned. "Seriously?"

He frowned at her outburst. "What's wrong?"

She shook her head. "Just makes my life difficult. Whatever, I'll deal with it."

Cole shrugged, unconcerned with her objections. "It was the easiest way to explain the lack of interviews and quick hiring process. Companies like Zia don't just bring in people quickly. Normally, it takes four rounds of interviews, a meeting with a psychologist, and a background check."

He didn't mention that the background check had been performed. He kind of wished he'd done the psych evaluation too. Wondering what was going on behind those dark eyes of Miss Rodriguez during their first meeting had driven him crazy. And though her emotions were far more subtle this morning, he couldn't help but wish he knew how her mind worked. Maybe the intensive interviews the psychologists performed would give a bit more insight about the woman he'd invited to see behind the curtain of his company.

He would trust Miss Rodriguez because Flint Raven trusted her. That was good enough for Cole.

"Patrick is a good guy. You'll like working for him," he said in an attempt to calm her nerves. "He's not a super technical computer guy, but he's good at managing a team."

"And what about you? Will I like working for you, Mr. Kensington?"

His breath caught at the way she said his name, like a secret shared between friends. He cleared his throat. "I don't see why that matters. Just do your job and we'll be just fine." He straightened his tie. "You'll find I don't concern myself with many things beyond my business."

She'd figure that out soon enough.

"You protect Zia, Miss Rodriguez, and I'll be your biggest fan. You betray me?" His jaw tensed at the thought. "I'll go to the ends of the earth to make sure you never work outside of a Best Buy again." He steeled his gaze, driving home the point.

Cole had dedicated his entire life to his goal. Ending up as the CEO of the company hadn't been in his plans, but being the CEO gave him decision-making power he'd never have as a researcher or manager. And, of course, the personal money to make things happen.

She stiffened at his words, jerking her chin upward. He pushed away the desire to reassure her. Of what, though? He wasn't joking. Twenty-five years of work had led him to a place where he could change the world, and he wasn't going to let Miss Rodriguez or anyone else jeopardize it.

"Do you understand?" he asked, doubling down on his attempt to make her understand just how serious he was about this job.

She held his gaze, apparently unbothered by his intimidation tactics. "Perfectly," she responded in a clipped tone, no expression revealing her true feelings. Not fear or admiration, the two emotions he was used to seeing on the faces of those he worked with. No, she wasn't scared of him. And she definitely didn't admire him. She almost seemed to hate him.

Which was fine. He wasn't here to make friends.

# CHAPTER
# THREE

JOEY SUCKED in a deep breath of fresh air when she was released from the town car. It was as if the small space had been designed to flaunt Kensington's wealth and power. Sitting there made every difference between the two of them blatantly obvious to her. He was supremely confident, almost arrogant in how he controlled the conversation. Her hands were still shaking slightly from the confrontation. They were supposed to be on the same side. At least, he was supposed to think they were.

She ground her teeth together, remembering the threat about banishing her to Best Buy. She'd figure out how to respond to that comment later. For now, she was actually proud she'd managed to bite her tongue. Digging into Cole Kensington would be far easier if she could get him to trust her–even if she'd never trust him. She probably should have been less confrontational at dinner. Maybe he'd be less guarded. But she couldn't change that now.

She walked the two blocks to the office after he dropped her off so no one would see them arriving together. Whatever she could say about Kensington, he wasn't stupid.

Joey pulled out her phone and texted Flint a quick update.

Joey: Headed in for day one. No phones allowed. I'll check in at lunch.

Flint: Be careful.

She deleted the messages and tucked her phone away before stepping into the building. She tried her best to appear as an enthusiastic but nervous computer tech on her first day. Employees trickled in around her, flashing their badges and proceeding through four sets of doors leading out of the lobby. In the center was a large reception desk. It was a safe bet that it was where she should start.

She tightened her grip on her shoulder bag and strode to the desk, chin high and eyes forward.

"Good morning. What can I do for you?"

Joey glanced briefly to the left and right of the friendly receptionist. Overweight and balding, the uniformed security guards seemed to be more for show than anything. They had radios on their belts, though. Surely, there were others behind the scene. Perhaps ones with more muscle.

She smiled warmly. "Hi. Um, it's my first day. I'm supposed to report to Patrick Wragge, I think?" She feigned ignorance and added a bit extra flightyness to her persona. It never hurt to be underestimated.

The receptionist brightened. "Oh, well! Welcome to Zia. Let me just call Patrick and see where you should go first. Usually, it's straight to HR for a few hours of paperwork." The middle-aged woman rolled her eyes. "Gotta keep the paper-pushers happy, don't we?"

Joey smiled. "Every company seems to have that in common."

"Hi, Patrick. It's Lisa at the front desk. I have–" She looked at Joey. "What was your name, honey?"

"Joey–I mean–Josephina Rodriguez."

The receptionist repeated her name. "I'll sign her up and send her to Tammy. Thanks." She turned back to Joey. "You'll need to lock your phone, smart watch, and any other Bluetooth-enabled device in those lockers over there." Joey's gaze followed the path of Lisa's gesture to the lobby wall. She hadn't noticed how many employees were stopping at the sleek-looking lockers to put their devices inside.

Tammy turned out to be a curvy blonde with glasses and a keen ability to talk non-stop for nearly four hours. By the end of the one-on-one orientation marathon, Joey's brain was ready to melt from the mundane chatter and the mind-numbing paperwork. During the review of the employee handbook, she briefly wondered if Black Tower even had one, smiling at the thought of what Flint would come up with for guidelines.

"We're almost all done here, and then I'll deliver you to Patrick myself. He's a great guy. You're so lucky to be in his department. Honestly, half the single women in the building have a little crush on him. Well, if they aren't harboring delusional thoughts about making Mr. Kensington fall in love with them. You'd think they did nothing but read cheap romance novels about the prince falling for the peasant girl and whisking her away to his castle."

Joey laughed at the accurate assessment. Miranda loved those books, much to her dismay. Joey'd take a good space opera any day. Or a Marcus Warner adventure thriller. If it weren't for the whole working with the "evil empire" thing, she might begrudgingly admit that Cole was handsome. Even then, there was

the unavoidable fact that he'd made his fortune prof-
iting from drug monopolies. She knew firsthand how
they took advantage of people who were unwillingly
dependent on them to survive. Of course, most girls
probably saw the money as a perk, not an absolute
dealbreaker. "You don't think Mr. Kensington would
do that?"

Tammy laughed. "Have you met the man? Sure,
he's handsome. But he's not interested in anything if
it doesn't have to do with Zia and the research
foundation."

Joey filed away that information. If there had ever
been any gossip about the boss, Tammy would have
heard it. And she seemed one-hundred-percent willing
to share it to the newest employee. She was exactly
the well-connected type of person who knew just
about everything happening inside of Zia.

"Research foundation?" Joey was going to take
advantage of Tammy's loose lips and get as much
insider information as possible. Plus, Tammy would
be a good friend to have. Having someone inside
Human Resources could be helpful.

Tammy leaned forward. "Oh yes. You'll learn
more about it next week during the official new-hire
bootcamp, but Zia not only conducts in-house
research, but we are also the sole sponsor of the Zia

Promise Foundation. ZPF sponsors university research grants, prescription assistance, and scholarships for bioscientists, medical researchers, and geneticists."

Joey let her admiration show. Even she couldn't pretend she wasn't impressed by what Tammy said about the non-profit side of Zia. "Wow, that's pretty great."

She couldn't let herself get too carried away with positive feelings for Kensington. It was probably all for the tax write-off. There, a nice cynical thought to balance out the admiration trying to weasel its way in.

Tammy nodded emphatically. "Yeah, it really is. I know sometimes our industry gets a bad rap. But once you are inside, you really see how much everyone is doing because we want to help. And Mr. Kensington takes it very seriously."

Joey thought back to this morning. Saying that he took it seriously might be an understatement. She didn't have a problem with protecting the things that were important or prioritizing accordingly. But she also liked to find joy where she could. Sometimes, working at BTS meant dealing with some pretty tough situations. Like stalkers trying to kill her boss's sister. Or a kidnapper demanding ransom for the return of an innocent little girl. But that didn't stop

Joey from decorating her desk with trolls or playing Disney music while she hacked into the personnel records of a Fortune 500 investment firm.

"Come on, Joey. I'll show you around and deliver you to Patrick–just in time for him to buy you lunch on your first day. Who knows, maybe you'll be the one to win his heart!" Tammy winked, and Joey gave a weak smile. That was the last thing Joey would be thinking about.

Tammy walked her through the main areas of the Zia Pharmaceuticals headquarters. In the basement, they watched through glass windows as researchers in white coats worked on things that Joey couldn't even pretend to recognize. Tammy scanned her badge at nearly every door they walked through, and pointed to even more that were restricted to them both.

Joey pretended to be surprised. "Pretty tight security, huh?" She recognized the system from her time at Raven Tech. Raven had made his fortune developing security solutions that were cutting edge. And she'd been with him every step of the way.

Tammy chuckled at Joey's casual observation.

"You could say that. Everything is locked up to everyone except the teams who work there. I've worked here for seventeen years, and there are entire floors in this building I've never seen."

They turned down another hallway. "I feel like I'm going to get lost," Joey said with a nervous laugh.

Tammy smiled. "You'll be fine. We've got maps. And you can always ask anybody for help. You're working for Patrick, which means you'll be on the fourth floor with the rest of the tech squad. Just find an elevator, swipe your badge, and hit the button for four." She shrugged. "Or you could find the stairs, but I can't help you there. I'm sure you would be unsurprised to find out I avoid the stairs as often as possible." Tammy ran her hand downward in front of her, gesturing to her waist and thighs.

"You obviously don't need them. You're gorgeous, Tammy."

Tammy blushed at the compliment. "I can see we're going to be friends already, Joey."

Joey smiled, "I think so, too." A twinge of guilt flashed through her mind. Lying never sat well with her, but what else could she do while undercover? Friendships didn't survive assignments like this.

"Here we are. Fourth floor. Technology Services."

Tammy led her toward what Joey assumed was Patrick's office, quickly confirmed by a glance at the nameplate as Tammy knocked.

Patrick stood, and Joey quickly appraised her new boss. Tall and fit, a touch of gray around his temples was the only indicator that the man was probably close to forty. He wore one of those golf shirts with fabric that was far too thin. Didn't they make undershirts for that sort of thing?

She held out her hand to shake his.

"You must be Josephina. I've heard so much about you." When he smiled, Joey could see what Tammy was talking about. He had that Dennis Quaid look.

Very charming.

"Please, call me Joey. And only good things, I hope," she said with a smile, easily falling into the game of corporate small-talk.

"Joey it is, then. Thanks for bringing her up, Tammy. I've got it from here."

Tammy promised to check in later in the week, making Joey laugh by pointing at Patrick and fanning her face when he wasn't looking.

After Tammy left, Patrick waved her farther into his office. "Come on in, have a seat. I want to get to know my newest specialist. Cole didn't tell me much about you."

"Oh? I thought you'd heard so much about me?"

Patrick's smile faltered slightly, and Joey wished she hadn't called him on the inconsistency. She quickly backtracked. "Sorry, sometimes I speak before I think. What do you want to know?"

The smile returned to her new boss's face, but Joey could tell it was measured. "Cole said you were a family friend and that you have some computer experience. I don't even think I've seen your resume," he said, his earlier friendly demeanor replaced with obvious annoyance. "I'm skeptical about what Cole calls computer experience. He's not exactly one of us."

Hadn't Cole said Patrick wasn't especially technical? Joey pretended to be embarrassed. "I still can't believe Cole just handed me the job. All I asked for was an interview! I'm so sorry to just be thrown in your lap." She reached into her bag and pulled out the resume she'd crafted over the weekend.

"As you can see, I worked for many years at Raven Tech and then as a freelancer." It was better to keep things as close to the truth as possible. "But the self-employed gig wasn't for me. I can do just about anything you need. Websites, cyber security, systems or database work. What can you tell me about your department?"

Patrick leaned back in his chair. "Raven Tech, huh? We use their integrated system, so maybe you won't be completely lost here. This whole department falls under the umbrella of technology. We've got the Marketing Technology folks who handle our customer facing website, phone apps, surveys, and digital advertising."

Maybe he came from a marketing background. That would explain his charismatic demeanor.

Patrick continued while Joey tried to keep it all straight. "Then there is the Database Management team and the standard IT staff, who are both pretty self-explanatory. Then we have the Internal Technology Security team. They work closely with the security personnel, but handle all of our security hardware—cameras, locks, key codes." He waved his hand as if to say et cetera. "As well as our internal network and server security, and cyber security for anything connected to external networks."

He tipped his chin down and gave her a serious look. "The work we do is important, and discretion and secrecy are critical to our success. This is the big time. I don't need a little leaguer on the team."

He just had to go with sports metaphors. Joey wanted to grimace at the condescension, but instead she smiled and nodded. "I totally understand. I'm happy to do whatever you need. I saw the job posting, but I'm a team player."

"Right. The job posting. That happened pretty

fast. Unusually fast." He shook his head. "Not that I'm complaining about the extra hands, but I like to choose my own staff. For now, we'll just have you shadow Ben Parker. Not that I don't believe your skills," he said with a smile that told Joey that was exactly why he was doing it, "but this way he can get you up to speed. And make sure you don't break anything. Cole might have stuck you in my department, but it's still my department and I make the calls."

Forget being underestimated. If she had any hope of not being fired, she was going to have to win Patrick over very quickly.

The entire speech told Joey everything she needed to know. Patrick assumed she was going to be a drain on the department. She'd be lucky if she got access to anything remotely classified. How could she play this to her advantage?

She smiled tightly. "I look forward to proving myself a valuable member of the team." What she was looking forward to was throttling Kensington for sticking her into this situation. Couldn't he have looped Patrick in? He claimed to trust the man, but apparently not enough to reveal her mission. Which meant Joey was going to spend every minute with a babysitter named Ben.

When they left his office, Patrick introduced her to her new guard dog. Ben Parker was a kid in his mid-twenties and seemed completely unconcerned with his new role as her instructor.

Then he showed her to her glass-walled cubicle, the empty desk a little jarring. A sleek chair sat in front of it, but otherwise there was nothing on the clear surface. Not even a spare pen or forgotten slip of paper. Not exactly a great place to do sleuthing into the servers.

"I told you I didn't know you were coming, so just order whatever hardware you need and have it delivered. Ask Ben for the account info."

When she dragged the ordering information out of Ben, who was reluctant to even remove his headphones, she chuckled at the Best Buy Corporate Account card. Well, at least this would be fun.

# CHAPTER
# FOUR

JOEY RETRIEVED her phone from the tiny locker using her fingerprint and waved good-bye to her new coworkers. She walked out of the Zia building just after five o'clock. Despite the overwhelming push of the corporate culture, most people seemed to be keeping relatively normal hours. Probably not Cole. At least not if his weekend emails were any indicator.

Her phone chimed with messages from several people as soon as she turned it on.

Flint: Report?

Ryder: How's the new gig?

Ryder: Do you still think he's part of the Syndicate?

Tank: I need a background check on a new housekeeper.

Unknown: We'll meet tonight. 8 pm. I'll pick you up.

She debated calling a ride share, but instead, she headed to the Metro station. How typical that Kensington had picked her up this morning and not bothered to care about how she got home.

"Miss Rodriguez!"

She turned and saw Cole's driver standing next to a black town car pulled over on the shoulder.

Oh great. She considered pretending she hadn't seen the driver. She'd seen Kensington's text. Had he changed his mind about the time of their meeting? She'd rather have some time before she had to face him again. Putting on airs for the entire day and sitting through a mind-numbing department staff meeting this afternoon on top of the orientation had drained her entirely.

"What does he want now?"

The driver's lips twitched, but he didn't smile fully. "Mr. Kensington is not in the vehicle, but he has asked me to see you home safely, since he left you without transportation."

Her irritation faded. That was... nice of him? Thoughtful, even.

She didn't like it.

"I'm fine. I'll take the Metro."

The driver softened his tone and tipped his head

toward his shoulder. "Please, I insist. The bar has been stocked with Mountain Dew at Mr. Raven's recommendation."

Her eyebrows shot skyward. "Mr. Kensington asked Raven what my favorite soda is?"

The driver fidgeted. "Well, no. That was my doing, ma'am. Please get in the car."

Joey sighed, already moving toward the van in surrender to the sweet siren call of the caffeine-loaded beverage. "Hey, kids, I've got some candy in my van," she said in an exaggerated deep voice. "Fine. I feel like I should know your name, though. I keep calling you Jeeves in my head, but that's probably rude."

He smiled. "My name is Jared, ma'am."

"Nice to meet you, Jared," she said, holding her hand out.

"Likewise, ma'am." Jared shook her hand and then stepped aside so she could climb in.

She paused, one hand on the top edge of the door. "Call me Joey."

"Yes, ma'am," he replied with another smile.

Joey settled into the luxurious seats and pulled an icy Mountain Dew from the cooler built into the console between seats. She could get used to this—when Kensington wasn't in the car with her.

She pulled her phone back out and began responding to texts, starting with Flint.

Joey: All clear. Headed to BTS now.

Then she responded to Ryder and Tank.

Joey: I'm sure of it. It'll be a long assignment though.

Joey: Seriously, Tank? Another one?

She could only laugh. This was the third housekeeper Tank had gone through in the last two months. He responded right away.

Tank: Ryder thinks they're scared of me. I think I'll try to avoid seeing this next one in person.

Joey: If that's true, it's ridiculous. You're a teddy bear...One who can kill a man with his bare hands. But a teddy bear, nonetheless.

Joey's heart surged with sympathy for Tank. He might come across as gruff and uncommunicative, but once you gave him a shot, he was perhaps the most loyal, kind man she'd ever met.

"Hey, Jared? Could you take me to–" She clamped her mouth shut. She'd been about to ask him to drop her off at Black Tower Security. But if Jared didn't know who she was, and she assumed he didn't, that wouldn't work. She searched for another option and spotted a billboard. "The Screaming Peach?" she finished lamely.

She saw Jared's eyebrow raise in the rearview mirror, but he didn't question it. "Yes, ma'am."

She smiled tightly. "Thanks. They have the best lemonade." The bookstore and cafe chain wasn't exactly what she needed, but at least it was on the way home.

Peach lemonade in hand, she waved good-bye to Jared and opened the door to her apartment building. After he'd driven off, she went back outside and drove her own car to BTS. This sneaking around part was ridiculous. No more fancy car rides from Jeeves. As much as she'd enjoyed the peace and quiet.

It was after six when she arrived at BTS, which meant Dolores was gone. The retired CIA field operative was Flint's favorite misdirect. While she was friendly and welcoming, she was also shrewd and capable of handling herself if things were ever to heat up at BTS headquarters. Joey swiped her access badge to enter the building and used her handprint to get beyond the lobby into the employee-only area.

Joey ran a hand along the edge of her largest computer monitor. "Hey, baby, did you miss me?" Dropping into her seat, she let out a sigh. This was home. And after spending all day in the uptight corporate cage with no access to a phone, computer, or her bag of tricks, she was ready for the second phase of her day. She turned on her music, dimmed the lights, and quickly lost herself in the tasks at hand.

"What in the world?" she mused out loud. She was layers deep into Kensington's finances. Mostly, it seemed on the up-and-up. Charitable donations were easily tracked, but there was a string of transactions she couldn't understand. In Kensington's accounts, there were contributions to a trust with no charitable standing that she could find. In fact, the trust documents were completely sealed, so she couldn't see anything about what was happening inside the trust. She could see that money was being distributed from the trust, but she couldn't see who the payments were being made to. Maybe the Syndicate was using these blind trusts to move assets around? The potential implications flooded her mind, giving her a hundred more leads to follow.

"I brought you dinner."

Joey whirled at the sudden intrusion. Tank stood in the doorway, extending a Chinese takeout container. Joey's stomach rumbled in response. Once she got to know him, it amused her how his words and the tone were so mismatched. Tank was gruff and commanding, even when he was being thoughtful.

Reluctantly, she turned away from her computer. It would take a long time to find those documents.

She turned down the Disney songs playing from the small speaker on her desk. "Thanks. I probably should have eaten on the way here." As it was, the lemonade had given her a sugar rush strong enough to push her through the last hour of digging into the background on everyone she'd met today. Tammy, Jared, Patrick. A deep dive into their finances, background, family, and contacts was already helping her feel like she had regained the upper ground. And then she'd circled back to digging into Kensington.

Information was everything.

She took the takeout and gestured for Tank to grab a seat. "So, tell me about your new housekeeper."

He shrugged. "I don't know. All I've got is a name and a phone number. Someone recommended her in the neighborhood chat."

She scooped noodles into her mouth with the chopsticks and nodded. "I can work with that."

"How was day one undercover?"

She rolled her eyes. "I'm not a secret agent. It was fine. Boring corporate stuff mostly."

"You need backup?" His face didn't betray any of the kindness intended by the words.

She smiled at him and considered the offer. It would be nice to have an ally inside Zia. Someone she could trust. Especially since the one person she was supposed to trust was the one person she trusted the least. So far, she didn't feel threatened at all.

"Not yet, but I promise to let you know if I do."

Tank grunted and then left without so much as a good-bye. She chuckled and continued eating as she wrapped up the background checks.

Joey checked the time in the corner of her computer display. She grabbed her phone from her bag and winced at the text from Kensington.

Unknown number: We're at your place.

Unknown number: Where are you?

Unknown number: Headed to BTS.

The last message was ten minutes ago. Which meant he was–

"Joey!" Flint's voice carried from the other end of the hallway, and telltale footsteps told her he was headed her way.

She turned to her computers. "Yeah, boss?" she asked over her shoulder.

"You have a visitor."

She turned. "Oh, Mr. Kensington. Nice to see you," she said with insincere sweetness.

"Why weren't you at your house?" he practically growled. "I texted you about tonight."

Her chair scraped against the floor as she jumped to her feet. This man was beyond infuriating. She ground her teeth and stepped forward, deliberately closing the space between them. Her heart was racing, but she refused to let her adrenaline betray her. She didn't love confrontation, but something about his arrogant demeanor coupled with her own thoughts about his allegiances just set her off.

She took a deep breath and spoke with a determined iciness. "Next time you want a meeting, you may request one. You *may ask*," she emphasized by punctuating each word, "when or where is convenient. I do not respond to being summoned like a low-paid assistant, desperate to please you. After an entire day of orientation and tours and not a moment of access to a computer, I had work to do." She gestured broadly to her office. "So here I am. Doing my job. If you don't like it, you are welcome to take it up with my boss." She glanced at Flint, who was watching the exchange with amusement. "Otherwise, you are welcome to sit down, and I'll catch you up on what I know."

Kensington looked back and forth between her and Flint, who simply shrugged. Cole sighed and stepped inside her office.

Flint reached in and patted his friend on the shoulder, making her throat close up. She hated that they were friends. "Have fun. I have a call, otherwise I'd join you. Joey, catch me up later, okay?"

She met her boss's eyes. He looked pointedly at Kensington and mouthed a command to be nice. Joey responded by pointing to herself as though offended he would feel the need to remind her. Flint walked away, and she blew out a breath, steeling herself for this encounter and thinking about Flint's reminder. Didn't he know? She was always nice–except to evil, greedy CEOs who were trying to pull one over on her most trusted friend.

# CHAPTER
## FIVE

COLE STUDIED the large office as he stood awkwardly in the center. It was dark, but there was enough light coming from screens and other equipment to see. Even the keyboard was lit up with rainbow LEDs. A low sound he couldn't identify hummed just over the noise of the computers. Was that... kids' music?

He found the source of the sound and then hit the button on the small speaker to turn it up. He recognized the music from *Cinderella* and turned to Joey. She glared at him, silencing his question. She sat down in a chair that resembled a starship captain's and set her Chinese food aside. It was nearly eight-thirty. Did she always eat so late?

She hit a few buttons on the keyboard, and the music stopped.

"Does Jared know I work for BTS?" she asked, a chilliness in her tone he was becoming all too familiar with.

He jerked slightly. That wasn't what he'd expected to be asked. "I'm not sure. We were at your house. We came here instead, though I didn't tell him why we were coming here." He answered the question honestly, speaking as the answer occurred to him. He hadn't even considered what Jared knew or didn't. "I imagine he assumes we're dating. Though he would never ask, nor would he tell anyone," he clarified.

He reached under his collar, suddenly tight at the idea of dating this unpredictable woman. It would never work. "Don't worry about it."

"He's probably the closest to you and your biggest security risk. How much do you know about him?"

Cole shook his head. "It's not Jared. He's like a brother to me."

Joey raised an eyebrow. "Brothers betray brothers all the time. How do you know him?"

He tensed. It was none of her business how he knew Jared. Like he was going to tell her about how he'd met Jared after his grandparents died. "I just do," he snapped. "I trust him. He respects my secrets. If I need to loop him in, I will."

Joey paused. "You trust him that much?" Her question was quiet, her voice slightly husky, and it disarmed his anger.

He unclenched his fists and nodded. "With my life."

Joey tilted her head, seeming to weigh that response. "Okay. Well, you have to know his background check had some major red flags." She clicked through a few screens on her computer.

Cole felt the resurgence of the anger at her intrusion into his life. His voice hardened, edged with steel. "You had no right to run his information." How much had she found about Jared's past? Did she know about the man Jared attacked? Or why he'd done it?

Joey whipped her chair around. "Do you want me to protect your precious company? Your precious research? Then I will do everything I can. I will trust no one." She spoke with raw bitterness, and he felt a pang of regret at his treatment of her. She was just trying to help. Then she leaned closer, and he stopped breathing, afraid to break the connection. "And I will verify every potential threat. Even the ones you might be blind to. Got it?"

He'd seen a glimpse of this confident passion this morning, but nothing like this. He broke their eye contact and nodded with a sigh. He rubbed a hand down his face and leaned back in the chair, creating much-needed distance from her. "Thanks. I know I've got a blind spot somewhere, otherwise I would have figured this out by now. But the idea that it could be Jared… It's just not an option for me. I know his background. I still trust him."

Joey's voice was quieter when she spoke again. "I get it. Sometimes, family isn't born, it's forged by choice in the fire of trial. Those bonds are stronger than blood. Especially when our own family isn't around." Her tone was full of melancholy, calling to him.

He pulled his gaze back to hers, wondering who she was talking about. She was an enigma–a mysterious tangle of layers he wanted to peel back one at a time. "That's exactly it," he agreed, thinking of Jared. Several moments of silence passed until his thoughts circled back to her. She mentioned family of choice. Who had she chosen as her family?

"What's your story, Joey?" The question came out before he could stop it.

She bristled, and he kicked himself for going too far. "Let's just get to work. For now, keep Jared in the dark, okay? I want to talk more about the project you're concerned about."

Cole pushed aside his foolish thoughts about untangling Joey Rodriguez. She was a distraction he couldn't afford. "Right. While Zia Pharmaceuticals is performing groundbreaking research on multiple fronts, our biggest goal is to make Alzheimer's and dementia preventable and curable diseases." He had explained this mission so many times, it was a well-practiced speech. But this wasn't a talk with investors or a polite chat with a stranger at a fundraiser.

Joey needed more.

"Across the industry, we've had limited success with treatment options. We can slow the progress of the disease. But we can't stop it." He leaned forward, knowing that what he was about to tell her was the biggest secret. "Zia has something promising on the prevention side, though. An experimental gene protein therapy that targets three of the common gene mutations that we know result in Alzheimer's-indicative structures in the brain."

Joey was watching him carefully, her eyes wide and luminescent in the blue glow of the computers.

"Long term, it's basically the equivalent of an Alzheimer's vaccine for at-risk people."

"Whoa."

He grinned. "I know! It wouldn't catch every case of the disease, but it has the potential to be incredible. And I'm throwing everything behind it based on the initial trials."

"But?"

He released a heavy sigh. That had been the good news. Now it was time for the bad news. "But we've had some security breaches. There are records of our data showing up offsite, and my team can't trace it. There are a few other labs suddenly testing similar therapies. I think there is someone leaking the information."

Joey's pink lips formed a thoughtful pout, and Cole tore his eyes away from them. "But why would they do that? And also, why would it matter? Shouldn't all your medical research people be sharing information anyway?" She pushed her hair out of her face. "Look, it doesn't matter to me. I'm sure all the money is in being the first one to solve the problem."

Cole was familiar with the argument. He shook his head to dispel the thought that it was about the profits. "I'm all for sharing information. But if someone takes information out of context, it could be really dangerous. I honestly don't care if another company cures Alzheimer's before us. It's not about the money. It's about the mission. And these other labs? Their results are completely different from ours, which makes ours look fake. Stealing information for any reason isn't exactly the mark of an altruistic entity, is it?"

Joey nodded. "Yeah, probably not. Okay, how do I get access to the servers for this project?"

Cole reared back. "What do you mean? I'm not giving you access."

Joey raised her eyebrow at him. "Cole, if the information you need protected is vulnerable, you're going to need my help to secure it."

He barely heard her words, his thoughts tripping on the way his name sounded on her lips. Had she called him Cole before? He didn't think so. Surely, he would have remembered the gut punch it carried.

He finally processed what she'd said. He couldn't even be upset she had talked to him like a kindergartner who needed the instructions repeated four times. "Sorry. You're right. Force of habit, I guess. I'm used to locking everything down. I'll make sure your employee ID has access to everything on site. There won't be an area you won't be able to enter— digitally or otherwise. Just don't touch anything in the labs, okay?"

She smirked. "You don't have to worry about that. If it doesn't have a hard drive or an Ethernet port, I'm not interested."

He briefly wondered if that sentiment extended to people.

"You need a ride home, Joey?"

The gruff voice came from the door, and Cole turned to the unwelcome visitor. Then he did a double take at the massive body standing in the entry.

"Hey, Tank. No, I've got my car, thanks."

Cole wondered briefly if the rejection would upset the huge man. He didn't sound happy offering the invitation, and he didn't look like the sort you wanted to cross.

Joey seemed unconcerned and simply waved good-bye. Tank stared at Cole for a moment and then looked back at Joey, ignoring him completely. "Who's the suit?" Cole stiffened reflexively at the treatment. He wasn't used to being ignored. Perhaps he was more accustomed to the special treatment his position and wealth afforded him than he realized. What was that verse? Pride goeth before a fall?

Joey chuckled, the silky waves of throaty laughter pulling away from his misplaced offense. "Good night, Tank. I'll call you tomorrow about that thing."

Cole wished he knew what they were talking

about. He couldn't help the curiosity about their relationship, and the way Joey smiled at the hulking man.

He cleared his throat when they were alone again.
"So, you really think you can find the leak?"

Joey nodded. "Yeah, I do. It's going to take me a
while to earn Patrick's trust." She made a face at him.
"Thanks for that, by the way. But I'll start snooping
around and see what I can find. What I'd like from
you is a list of names of people who have access to
the information. It's not out of the realm of possibility
that they are gaining access they shouldn't have, but
more likely, it is someone or several someones who
already have access."

Cole hadn't even considered the possibility that
there was more than one person responsible. "I'll get
you the list tomorrow morning."

Joey shook her head. "Okay. You have my BTS
email address. It's secure."

He nodded. "Okay."

Joey turned to him. "You sound nervous, Mr.
Kensington."

"Call me Cole." He couldn't explain why it was
important to him. Usually, he was content being Mr.
Kensington. Insisted on it, in fact. It kept the lines of
boss and employee clear. But Joey had made very
clear that he wasn't her superior.

"You sound nervous, Cole." A little thrill raced through his arm and to his chest. She continued, "I heard your warning this morning."

Warning? What warning?

"You shouldn't worry. I'm the *best. By* this time next week, we'll have your man."

There was a little emphasis within her words that made him pause. His brow furrowed.

Joey stood up and grabbed her leftovers. "Well, I'd *best buy* myself some groceries and head home."

His lip twitched. There it was again. Why was she… oh. The warning.

Why wasn't he surprised that she was turning his threat of unemployment into a joke and taunting him with it? He didn't know how to respond. Instead, he followed her lead and stood. Which brought them very close in the dark space. He met her gaze, wondering what she saw when she looked at him.

"I should—"

"Thanks for—"

Joey laughed and stepped away, pushing buttons on her keyboard that caused the monitors to go dark, leaving them completely ensconced in shadows. The large office instantly felt incredibly cramped. Once his eyes adjusted, the light from the hallway was enough to see, revealing the outline of her shape. He moved toward the door.

"I'll walk you out," he said.

"Is Jared out there?"

Cole nodded, and Joey shook her head in response.

"That's okay," she said. "I need to catch Flint before I leave anyway."

"Okay. We'll talk tomorrow." Her refusal made sense, but he didn't have to like it. He'd much rather spend another few minutes with her, though he didn't want to examine why.

Joey nodded and opened the door to the lobby of BTS with the touch of a button.

"Good night."

Cole climbed into his car and sat silently on the way home. Lost in thought. Thoughts about his company. The threat. Joey.

He needed to get a hold of himself. Joey Rodriguez might be beautiful, intelligent, and insightful, but he couldn't entertain any thoughts beyond her completion of the job he'd hired her for. His purpose was to serve at Zia and finally deliver a blow to the disease that had destroyed his family. Everything else had always been secondary. There were a dozen reasons he needed to stay focused–the least of which was the fact that she seemed to despise him, which meant it didn't matter anyway.

"Cole?"

He blinked then met Jared's eyes, full of laughter, in the mirror. "Everything okay?"

He realized Jared must have tried to get his attention several times. "What? Sorry. Just a lot on my mind." He looked back out the window, barely seeing the lights of Alexandria going past.

Jared nodded. "You take on too much, Cole."

Cole looked back at his friend and driver. "I don't have a choice. You know that."

Jared shook his head. "I know you think that, but it's not true."

Cole sighed. They'd had this argument too many times before to rehash it again. "I'll just go home now."

Jared pressed his lips into a firm line and nodded. Cole didn't have the energy to wonder or worry about what his best friend was thinking right now. He probably didn't want to know. It wasn't like Jared had room to judge. There was a reason he was working for Cole. Mistakes in his past that made his life more difficult now. Jared might be a convicted felon, but Cole meant what he said to Joey.

He trusted Jared with his life.

Which sometimes meant being confronted with his opinions of it.

Even if Cole didn't always like it.

# CHAPTER SIX

JOEY STAYED UP TOO LATE, staring at the ceiling and trying to wrap her mind around everything she'd learned from Mr. Kensington.

Cole.

The fact that Jared was a criminal was the biggest surprise. Aggravated assault though? She wouldn't have expected it. The guy seemed pretty decent. Maybe that was the Mountain Dew talking.

It shouldn't have surprised her though. If Cole Kensington was a member of the Syndicate, why wouldn't his personal bodyguard and driver have a criminal record? That was exactly the kind of muscle someone in the Syndicate would use.

Then again, she'd listened to Cole talk about his

research and vision for Zia, and it was hard to believe it was all an act. He seemed so passionate about the possibilities. Was it really all for money in the end? Or power? Just imagining the kind of influence the person who cured Alzheimer's would have was mind-boggling. He might get the Nobel Prize. Probably end up as an advisor for the White House or something. That kind of achievement opened up more than bank accounts.

Cole Kensington was a big player. But he wasn't a household name. But he would be. Maybe Syndicate members were hoping to get him elected at some point. He'd be a good politician. Handsome. Smooth. Smart.

He certainly appeared altruistic. She'd done some digging into his finances. The man was rich. Loaded, actually. But not as much as he could be. His salary as CEO was generous, but his charitable giving was excessive by most measures. And not just to his own foundation. The man basically dropped money toward every hospice and special needs foundation in Virginia and New York.

But what was Cole putting money into the trust for? And who was it paying out to? She hadn't gotten to follow those leads down tonight.

She rolled over and punched the pillow, trying to

make it more comfortable. She had to avoid the very real temptation to like him. In her office, she'd come dangerously close to spilling her secrets. That was the total opposite of the goal.

Goal number one: protect Black Tower.

Goal number two: unmask and take down the Syndicate.

The fact that Cole may or may not have started with a noble purpose was irrelevant. Somewhere along the way, he'd fallen into the trap of greed and ambition. And it was up to her to prove it. She couldn't ignore that there was now a third goal.

Goal number three. Find the mole inside Zia.

As much as it pained her to admit, it really sounded like Zia was doing good things. And if this gene therapy was as promising as Kensington thought, then she didn't want to have a part in its failure or sabotage. Just because Kensington as CEO might be corrupt didn't mean that the entire mission of Zia Pharmaceuticals was a lost cause.

And maybe she'd just leave herself a little extra access into their system so she could make sure Zia couldn't monopolize and cash in on the treatment once it was established. But first, she had to help him make sure it was fully developed and approved.

She was ironically both *on* Kensington's team and

firmly opposing him. If Cole was part of the Syndicate, then she had to watch her back. Because one wrong move would paint a huge target on it. She had the feeling that Cole would do anything to protect his "friendship" with Flint.

Well, she wasn't going to let her guard down. She'd help Kensington with his project. But at the same time, she was going to prove exactly what kind of person he was. In her last information sweep, she found that he owned a house in Key West. His next-door neighbor just happened to be Shane Derulo. The CEO of QuinTech Missiles had built his fortune on war and fearmongering for government contracts, and —if her intel was correct—paying off key people in the budget and purchasing arena.

His ties to Tripp Harrington, along with his connections to Senator Collins and Morris couldn't just be coincidental. But it was all circumstantial. This mysterious legal trust could be the key. There were also his mysterious ties to Jared.

Unless she could find something concrete, Flint was never going to listen to her.

But she was inside Zia now. And that meant she had access she'd never be able to get any other way. She just had to figure out how to take advantage of it.

The next day, she parked in the garage next to Zia and walked through the tunnel connecting the buildings. Her mission today was to get some uninterrupted access to the server room. As long as her computer came. She smirked. It would be far easier if she could sneak her own laptop in, but she knew that wasn't going to happen. Instead, she'd be working right under the nose of the ITS department, using equipment they'd paid for.

"Good morning, Ben."

Her cubicle neighbor looked up and jerked his head up in acknowledgement with a grunt. The oversized headphones appeared to be an ever-present fixture.

Okay then. Not a morning person. Or maybe just not a people person. "Do you have anything I can do before my computer arrives?"

Ben didn't respond, already looking down at his own system. She waved her hand in front of his face and then pointed to her ears when he looked. He pulled the headphones down. "What?"

"Hi. Hello. Nice to see you again, Joey. You too, Ben." She held the conversation with herself, saying his lines as well as hers. "I was wondering if you have any work I can do while I wait for my computer."

He rolled his eyes. "No."

She smiled tightly. "Great. I'm going to go get familiar with the server room, then. Do you want to show me around?"

Ben looked down. "You'll figure it out. Apparently, you've got quite the resume," he sneered.

Joey raised her eyebrows. So Ben was threatened by her? She wasn't sure if that was a good thing, but it sounded like it was going to make him leave her to her own devices to sink or swim.

She smiled tightly. "Okay, then. Great chat."

Ben pulled his headphones back on, and Joey sat back down at her empty desk. Her gaze fell on Ben's jacket, hanging on the hook between their cubes. She kept her eyes on him as she stood, palmed his access badge, and walked toward the server room. Her heart raced, and she waited for alarms to sound and the hulking security guards to appear out of nowhere and escort her out.

Instead, there was nothing. She glanced at Patrick's office, but it was empty. She glanced around the open room, but no one paid her any attention. She swiped the card at the door and entered the server room, shutting the door quietly behind her, shutting out the chatter of voices in the large office space.

Technically, her employee badge had full access. But she didn't want to raise any questions from the folks who monitored the security logs. Even with permission, the Raven Tech system would flag her access and require a confirmation approval from the onsite team. Easier to borrow Ben's badge for now.

The dark room, filled with racks and familiar green lights, returned Joey's pulse to normal. She shivered slightly at the cool air. She saw two terminal monitors, one on each rack and went over to one. The login screen came up when she tapped the keyboard. She frowned at it, then grabbed a flashdrive from her pocket. Her own creation, the program on the device should bypass the login screen.

She held her breath while the program ran and exhaled when it worked. She started poking around, familiarizing herself with the organization system. There were so many unfamiliar names and acronyms, it was going to take her days to know what she was looking at, let alone find the vulnerabilities. She found the email server, and her fingers itched to dive into Kensington's inbox.

The door to the server room opened, and she jumped.

"Joey?"

In the doorway, she saw a familiar face. "Oh, hey, Patrick."

"What are you doing in here?" Was it just her imagination or did he sound suspicious?

She quickly logged out. "Just trying to get the lay of the land. No computer yet… Ben said it was okay to come in here," she said cheerfully as she slid her USB from the terminal into her palm.

Patrick watched her for what felt like minutes. She forced herself not to say anything. She wasn't guilty. Her heart pounded in her chest. Surely, he could hear it, even over the hum of the cooling fans in the room.

Finally, he waved his hand toward the door. "We've got a team meeting. Let's go."

She nearly sagged in relief. Joey glanced back at the workstation as she followed him, wishing she had more time. Maybe she could stay late and dig some more. What would she find in those emails and call logs from Kensington's personal phone and email? It seemed the key to everything about him was somewhere in this room, stored in zeroes and ones. It was up to her to find it.

They walked past Ben's cube, and she paused to clip his ID card back on his jacket and return to her desk. "Let me just grab my notebook," she said to Patrick to cover the delay.

When Joey sat down in the meeting, she tried to disguise the deep breath of relief she took. It was stressful being covert. Even if she had the boss's permission. At least for most of it.

"Ben, can I get an update on the system updates for the RT800x system?"

"Raven Tech has scheduled the update for third quarter, if we approve of that time frame. It will be a phased implementation. They estimate the upgrade will take four weeks from kickoff to closeout."

Joey tried not to let her surprise show. Ben could carry on a conversation? And he was spearheading a project as major as the security system overhaul. Maybe she'd underestimated him.

Ben continued. "During this upgrade, Raven Tech will be upgrading all of our encryption technology for secure access points and badges, server security, and confidential network communication."

Patrick nodded. "What encryption are we using now?"

"We currently have 128-bit AES," Ben replied.

"Are we moving to 192 or 256?" Joey asked. Her curiosity and her desire to prove herself a valuable team member played equal parts in her jumping into the conversation.

Ben raised an eyebrow and exchanged a look with Patrick. "We're moving to 256. The executive team wants us to spare no expense in making our building and data as secure as possible."

"Do we have concerns that the loss of efficiency will be detrimental?" another team member chimed in.

Patrick gave a bewildered look and turned to Ben for the answer.

Ben shook his head. "Raven Tech has assured us there will be no loss in operational efficiency with the upgrade."

"Good, thanks, Ben. Good work. Keep us posted as the kickoff gets closer."

———

Cole raised his eyebrows as he approached his office to someone wheeling a dolly stacked high with boxes into the room. Bright-blue labeled Best Buy boxes, to be exact.

What on earth was going on? He glanced at his employee nametag and then reached for the packing slip. He tried to remember. Had he ordered something and forgotten about it? It was one of his biggest fears. He knew the odds, and he knew the early signs of the disease he was working so hard to prevent. Was it just forgetfulness? Or something more?

"I think there's been a mistake, Thomas. I didn't order–"

He looked at the labels, and the words died on his lips.

The broad-shouldered mailroom worker shrugged. "I just go where the paper says, Mr. Kensington. These have your name on them." Thomas stepped aside, and Cole took in the view of his office, stacked with close to thirty giant Best Buy boxes.

The corner of his lips twitched, and he shook his head. This woman was going to be the end of him.

"Take them downstairs, fourth floor."

"Seriously?" Thomas's voice took on a small whine, and Cole felt the twinge of sympathy for the man.

He clapped the young man on the shoulder. "Fine. Leave them here. This wasn't your fault. I'll have the culprit take care of it."

The relief was palpable on Thomas's face. "Thank you, Mr. Kensington. This already put me way behind on my rounds for the day."

Irritation flooded Cole once more. Joey might

think she was funny, but this was interfering with not only his day, which was unacceptable as it was, but she was also inconveniencing his other employees.

He turned to speak to Janet, his personal assistant. "Call Ms. Rodriguez in ITS and have her come to my office immediately."

Janet raised her eyebrows at the clipped command but reached for her phone. At least some people listened to him. He hadn't forgotten what Joey said last night about being summoned like a low-paid assistant.

Well, Janet was definitely not low-paid. Perhaps he was a little short sometimes though.

"Thank you, Janet," he said as an afterthought.

She gave him a look of surprise, which made him feel even worse. Maybe Joey had a point.

Cole weaved through the towering maze of boxes that now filled his usually sparse and spacious office. He clipped one of the boxes with his hip and sent the tower tumbling into the stack next to it. A frown crossed his face. It barely felt like there was anything in the box. He picked one up and shook it to hear the faintest rattle inside.

He chucked the box into the corner, taking out some of his frustration out on the package. Then he sat at his desk and tried to focus. His gaze kept coming up to the mess of boxes in the space. It was impossible to concentrate in this mess.

He punched the intercom on his phone. "Janet, when will Ms. Rodriguez be here?"

"My name is Joey."

The low, almost sultry voice had him jerking his eyes to the doorway. She looked incredible today. Yesterday, her hair had been straight, falling in front of her eyes during their entire conversation. Now, it was curly and barely restrained in some sort of messy jumble just behind her ear.

He cleared his throat. "Ms. Rodriguez, what is the meaning of this?"

Joey's mouth curled up in a wicked smile. "Oh my. Did my order come to your office instead? What a strange mistake. I'm sure I put my name and office on the order information."

He narrowed his eyes. "Why are there so many boxes?"

She looked around. "You know, I don't really know. I ordered a computer and some pens and sticky notes and such. I can't imagine they would ship each item individually, can you?"

Her voice was full of innocence and confusion. And Cole wasn't buying any of it.

"You did this," he stated with absolute certainty.

Her hands flew to her chest. "Me? What do you think, that I somehow got into the inventory and shipping software inside of Best Buy's system and changed the settings on each item I ordered to ship in its own oversized box, just for the pleasure of inconveniencing you? Why would I do such a thing?" Her eyes were wide and her tone full of exaggerated sweetness.

"Joey," he growled in warning. He didn't have time for this. Didn't have time for the way she was making him feel.

She crossed her arms in front of her. "Cole," she replied without any trace of the innocent act.

He paused at her refusal to back down. Why wouldn't she back down? She had turned one comment from him into an absolutely ridiculous display of her skills. Skills that he admittedly needed. As much as he hated to admit it, she was right to be upset about his words yesterday. "I'm... sorry I said that about your job."

She raised her eyebrows, as though waiting for him to continue.

"Obviously, I got a little carried away." He shook his head. "And you have proven yourself to Flint. I heard what you said last night. You're the right person for this job."

Joey took a few steps forward. "Darn right I am. I'm going to be pressing into things you might not like. Asking questions you would rather not answer. But I need you to be completely honest with me, because while you might trust me because of Flint, I haven't decided if I trust you."

He reared back in surprise. "What? Why not?" That didn't even make sense. He was the one who was revealing all kinds of proprietary information to her. He was the one who needed to trust her. She didn't even have any skin in the game.

"That's my business. Just don't keep secrets and we'll be just fine. And don't threaten me again, Cole. You'll find a prank like this is the least of what I could do to you, okay?"

Everything within him resisted the power struggle between them. He liked being the one in charge. He liked being the one calling the shots. But where had that gotten him. As much as he hated to admit it, he needed her—someone from the outside. Someone trustworthy.

She didn't trust him? "I don't have anything to hide," he said firmly.

"We'll see about that."

He frowned. "Your job is to find the leak. I don't see what I have to do with that."

"Mr. Kensington–"

"Cole," he corrected.

"We'll find the leak. But I need your help," she said simply. "The fact is, you're the key to everything that happens in this company."

# CHAPTER
## SEVEN

JOEY TOOK A SEAT, drumming her feet on the floor as she leaned forward to share her idea. It had come to her while sitting in the insufferably long meeting with Patrick and the rest of the Technology Division before she'd been summoned to Cole's office anyway. Technically, she hated being summoned, but in this case it had been a rescue more than anything. The meeting was Patrick's information sharing meeting, passing along updates from other departments and from the executive staff, and getting updates on ongoing projects.

Every Tuesday afternoon, he gathered the entire division and they shared anything new.

Joey could understand the purpose of the meeting, but sitting through it was pretty torturous. Especially since she wasn't a real employee. She'd actually been on the edge of falling asleep when Jan's call had interrupted.

Right now, though, she was buzzing with energy. "I want you to be ready to send a memo to your team of directors, hinting at a big development in the research along with whatever other normal updates you give. Tell them to disseminate the information like they normally would–meetings or emails."

She'd spend some additional time tonight in the server to get some details together. Then she and Cole would lay a trap. With some strategic memos, some false test results, and a little program to sniff out the culprit, she was fairly confident it would work. "Basically, we want to lay the groundwork that there is something big going on. The mole won't be able to resist. When someone bites, we'll know who it is."

Cole pursed his lips in thought. "What if no one takes the bait? If they know the results are fake?"

She pursed her lips and jerked a shoulder. "Then they must be exceptionally close to the research. Close enough to know that you are making it up."

Cole drummed his fingers on the desk. "What if the note to the research team is a little different? Something about successful external trial results?"

Now they were talking. She didn't get too much of the collaborative problem solving in her role at BTS. This was kind of fun. "Yes, that could work really well. They'll make a ton of noise in the system trying to track down a fictional trial." Her mind was racing, thinking of everything she would need to get in place for the trap to work. "I need a week or two to lay the groundwork. I'll keep you posted." She grinned at Cole, unable to hide her enthusiasm about the plan.

Cole nodded. "You're dismissed."

Her smile faded instantly at his words.

Dismissed? It was a bit like the principal's office. There was no doubt Cole Kensington was used to being in charge, commanding each meeting he took part in. "I'll go when I'm ready," she replied cheekily, letting her smile return and challenging him to push her away again.

Cole leaned to look around her, and she turned to follow his gaze. The huge pile of boxes came into view as she turned. A laugh nearly escaped.

Did he realize how funny she was?

Judging by the look on his face, he didn't. That was a shame. Someone needed to lighten him up.

But not her. Definitely not her.

She flushed at the realization that she had essentially been flirting with the man she was investigating. Secretly. While pretending to be his ally.

She needed to get a grip. She was not his type. More importantly, he wasn't *her* type. Who wanted someone handsome, successful, and generous anyway?

Not her. Especially when it came with a side of dishonesty and corruption.

He raised an eyebrow and looked at her expectantly. "Take your things and go, Miss Rodriguez. You've got work to do, remember?"

Drat. Kensington was right. No matter how much more fun it would be to stay here and ruffle his feathers—or better yet, start putting things in place for their trap—she did have things to do. Especially if she was going to have late-night access to the server room. She wouldn't be able to steal Ben's access card after hours.

Making as much noise as possible, she gleefully ripped into a box and pulled out the package of pens inside. Then she repeated the process with each box, finding all the paperclips and notebooks—and computer equipment—she had ordered. She couldn't help but chuckle. No matter what stick was up Cole's rear end, this was funny.

While she worked, Kensington never said a word,

but she felt his eyes on her every minute of the task. As she retrieved her items from their hilariously over-sized packages, she broke down the boxes and stacked them neatly near the entry of his office.

She slid her hand along the seam of a box after she slit the packing tape. A sharp stinging made her jerk her finger away. "Oh, ouch!" She dropped the scissors so she could squeeze her finger with the other hand.

When she tentatively pulled it away, blood rushed to the surface and out of the surprisingly jagged cut between the second and third knuckle of her index finger. A paper cut. Or cardboard cut. Whatever it was called, all she knew was that it hurt like the dickens.

In seconds, Kensington was by her side. She turned away reflexively. "Let me see," he said gently.

Joey held her injured finger close to her chest, squeezing tightly to relieve the pain. "I'm fine," she insisted. "Just a nick." It wasn't just a nick, but she wasn't going to let him see her as weak.

"Don't be stubborn, Joey." His voice was laced with exasperation and concern.

Reluctantly, she held it out and released her death grip.

Cole hissed when he saw the slice from the corrugated box. Okay, maybe it was worse than she thought. "Ouch," he said, reaching for a tissue from his desk. He gingerly dabbed at the wound, clearing away the excess blood. "That's a nasty one. It shouldn't need stiches though. Let me get you some antibiotic cream."

Joey grabbed the tissue he left and eyed him as he pulled out a drawer in his desk across the room. "You have a first-aid kit in your desk?" How many CEOs could say that?

He looked up from the small red case, triumphantly holding a small tube of ointment. "Of course."

"Let me guess. Boy Scout?"

He walked back over and smiled, but it didn't reach his eyes. "No, I promise, I'm no Boy Scout. Just like to be prepared. In case I need to take care of someone," he added, the velvety tenderness of his tone making her heart thunder in her ears.

He dabbed the ointment on her finger, his fingers impossibly gentle. She swallowed thickly, her own body betraying her.

"There." He finished wrapping a Band-Aid around the cut. "Feel okay?"

She nodded wordlessly. His compassion was killing her.

Death by a thousand cardboard cuts would be preferable to falling for someone like him.

At least, that was what she had to keep telling herself.

———

Cole trudged back into the lobby of Zia around eight o'clock that night. His dinner meeting with the FDA representative had edged on disastrous. They'd been pushing him for a new update on the Cognitive Protective Barrier—Protein Gene Injection, or CPB-PGI—gene therapy project for months, and he'd been putting them off. Because it wasn't ready to share. And until he could figure out how his research was being leaked, he couldn't come out and request approval for the next stage. Moving forward while he had a data leak was asking for trouble.

The FDA representative confirmed that other labs were reporting first-round data from similar approaches. She'd also confirmed that their results hadn't been good. Which didn't make sense. Everything he'd seen from his own internal results had been extremely positive. At least when he'd last received an update. One of the things he was headed upstairs to do was put things in place for a more formal update.

Either way, without an update to the FDA in the next two months, the FDA was going to shut down the CPB-PGI therapy project based on the results seen elsewhere. Which would put an end to the most promising prevention therapy he'd seen in decades of research. The other results were a lie. They had to be. Giving up on this wasn't an option. He just had to work harder.

He waved half-heartedly at the security guard at the front desk, then pulled his phone out of his pocket when it rang.

Flint's name displayed on the readout, so despite his foul attitude, he answered.

"Any chance this can wait until tomorrow?"

"Wow, that's quite a greeting. Do you answer everyone's calls that way, or was that especially for me?" Flint's good-natured ribbing brought a smile to Cole's face.

"Hey, you should feel honored that I picked up at all. It's been a day."

"I'm sorry to hear that. Anything I can do?"

Cole punched the number for the twelfth floor and sighed. "Not really, man. As long as Joey does what she's supposed to do."

Flint hummed. "And how's that going?"

Cole looked up at the ceiling. "She's something else, Flint. I don't know exactly what to make of her."

On the other end of the phone, Flint chuckled. "Yeah, that sounds about right."

"Why do you trust her so much?"

"We've been through the wringer together, you know? She means a lot to me. And I know she's been through a lot. She won't talk about it, but it makes it hard for her to trust people. But if you can get her on your side, you'll never find a better ally."

"And if she's not on my side?"

Flint let out a low whistle. "Well then, watch out. But you shouldn't have to worry about that."

Cole wasn't so sure. He remembered what she'd said in her office about her own reasons for not trusting him. What he couldn't figure out was what it might be. Was it just her own issues or something about him in particular?

"She played a prank on me today," he said plainly.

"Oh no," came Flint's reply.

"Oh, yes," he responded drily.

"I'm sorry, Cole. I should have warned her about you."

"About me? What does that mean?"

"It's just… you're a bit serious. Especially about work. I get it, obviously. But Joey? She's a firecracker. I should have warned her to tone it down. What did she do?"

Cole told Flint the story as he made his way down the dim, empty hallways toward his desk.

"You got off easy, Kensington. This morning, I had to borrow Miranda's laptop for a meeting because Joey somehow reprogrammed my keyboard so the keys were all mixed up. It was impossible. Luckily, she fixed it tonight. I had to bribe her with one of Fiona's cheesecakes."

Cole chuckled. "Bribery, huh?" Maybe he could bribe her, too.

"I'm a desperate man," Flint replied.

He threw his coat over the chair and spun around, facing the window and looking over the lights of Silver Spring's commercial center. "I know how you feel," he sighed the words.

"Can I pray for you, Cole? I should have done it the other night at Hamilton's, but I got caught up in the logistics of bringing Joey in."

Cole tipped back in his chair and looked up to the ceiling before closing his eyes in gratitude. He didn't know what he'd done to deserve a friend like Flint Raven, but God had really been gracious with that connection.

"That would be amazing," he said honestly, his

voice full of emotion. "This whole project and the ramifications are really weighing on me. I'm terrified we're going to lose the traction we've gained after all this time. It feels like it's all on me right now. I don't know if I can do it, Flint."

His throat closed up and he choked out the last few words. Admitting his struggle was harder than he imagined.

"I totally get it. I've been there. But don't forget that you're not actually the one in control. I know it's hard to live it out sometimes, but God's plan will come to pass with us or without us. We get the privilege to be a part of it sometimes, but it's not about us."

Cole wrestled with the words as Flint continued. "Sometimes, people underestimate their importance in God's plans. But guys like us?" Flint gave a small scoff. "We're just as likely to *overestimate* our importance and try to carry it all on our shoulders. It's too heavy to do that."

Cole leaned forward. "I know you're right. But I'm just trying to do what I know I'm supposed to do. This is it, you know? Everything I've been working for is right here. And I'm afraid it's going to slip out of my grasp."

"That's the hard part. If you don't end up with a

cure for Alzheimer's, but you end up closer to Jesus for having walked this path…" Flint let the pause linger before asking, "Will that be enough for you?"

Cole blew out a heavy breath. "Come on, Flint. That's not fair." He shook his head in denial. What kind of question was that?

"I know, I know. It sucks to think about. But I'm serious. What if all you have to show for it at the end of your life is Jesus. Isn't that everything?"

Cole shook his head. He knew the right answer was yes, of course. But his heart was screaming at him "no way!" That wasn't enough. Not for him. Not after all these years.

"I'm going to have to get back to you on that one, Raven."

"Can I just say…I'm glad you didn't say yes when you didn't mean it?" Flint's tone was kind and understanding.

"Yeah, yeah. You know me too well for me to even try to lie to you."

Cole fought back tears as Flint prayed over everything they had talked about. When they hung up, Cole's heart was lighter, just having talked to Flint tonight. Now it was time to get to work on the list of things he'd made on the drive from the restaurant to the office.

He would need to think about what his friend had said about the unthinkable what-if question. But while he thought about it, he was going to keep pushing to save his project. If what the FDA representative had said was true, he only had two months.

# CHAPTER
## EIGHT

JOEY SAT in Miranda's office, nibbling on the end of a piece of licorice as she caught Miranda up on everything that had happened.

"You did not ship thirty boxes to his office!" Miranda said through her laughter.

Joey wiggled the licorice through the air and shrugged. "Oh, I definitely did. But he deserved it."

The phone on Miranda's desk rang. She glanced at the caller ID before answering it on speakerphone.

"Hey, Jackson, what's up?"

"Hey, beautiful. I need a favor."

Joey raised her eyebrow at the endearment. Jackson drove her absolutely crazy with his larger-than-life ego. It seemed like he made it his mission in life to annoy her.

"What do you need? And just so you know, Joey's in here with me."

Jackson's tone brightened. "Hey, J-Rod. I thought you got fired?"

Joey glared at the phone. "We both know if anyone is getting fired, it's going to be you. And don't call me that."

He laughed. "Fine, fine. Since you asked so nicely."

Joey huffed at his arrogance, but before she could get snarky in return, Miranda was answering his questions, blushing as she assured him she could get what he needed.

"I'll send you the address of a safehouse in Houston. And I'll have that package waiting for you when you arrive."

Joey didn't know how Miranda made arrangements for things like housing, equipment, and vehicles magically arrive all over the country when Black Tower needed it, but she was a magician.

"You're amazing. Do me one last favor?"

Joey rolled her eyes. What else could the man possibly want?

"Sure, anything you need," came Miranda's breathy response.

"Look up the words brilliant and beautiful on that computer of yours."

Her friend leaned back with a grin on her face. "Oh, would you look at that? It's me," she replied cheekily.

Joey raised her eyebrows. Jackson was shameless.

"Gotta go, sweetheart."

The call disconnected, and Joey stared at her friend expectantly.

"What?"

"Are you two always like that?"

"Like what?" Miranda said.

"He is flirting with you like crazy!" Joey let her animated disapproval show.

Miranda shrugged. "Yeah, maybe. I'm flirting with him, too. But we're just friends. It's just fun, you know?"

Joey shook her head. "No, I don't know. Because, unfortunately, I talk to Jackson all the time. He has never once called me baby girl, princess, sweetheart, or beautiful."

Miranda shrugged. "I don't know what to tell you, Joey."

"Just be careful. If he hurts you, we're going to have a big problem."

"He won't," Miranda assured her. "It's not like I

think he means anything by it. I know better than that."

Did she though? Joey hoped so, because her friend was hilarious and confident, but Jackson was… well, he was the kind of guy that girls threw themselves at. The prom king and the football star. Miranda was quirky and colorful and entirely too good for him.

"If you say so, sweetie. I'll let you take care of whatever it was he needed. I've got to get a few more things ready before I head back to Zia later anyway."

"Be safe," Miranda urged her before she left.

Around ten p.m., Joey waved to the security guard at the front desk.

"Late night?" he asked.

She nodded. "No rest for the weary," she said with a friendly smile. She tapped her newly re-coded access card to open the lobby doors. Please work. Please work.

It flashed red and beeped once.

She tapped again. Red. Sweat beaded on her forehead.

She said a silent prayer. She'd taken her own access badge back to BTS and re-keyed the encryption to grant her full access. It hadn't been too difficult, since it was Raven Tech equipment she'd developed during her time working for Flint's Tech business. It was long before Black Tower Security, but the skeleton of his security technology still carried the company. And it was still the best.

The security guard stood up.

"Finicky cards. Probably due for a new one."

She moved the card toward the reader again. The light flashed green, and she opened the door with her back and smiled at the guard before hurrying toward the elevator. Her picture and information would still flash on his screen. But behind the scenes, in the access logs? There would be no record of Joey Rodriguez from the fourth floor being in the building.

In minutes, she was back in the server room. Her bag was full of tricks: a cellphone with no signal, to avoid being seen by the fortress-level signal detection system Zia used, a flashdrive that would leave no footprint, and several other programs that she could use to sniff out the things she was interested in.

First things first. Kensington's emails.

She searched through the text for familiar names. From Flint's first run-in with the Syndicate three years ago and Ryder's incident with them last spring, she'd been building a dossier on the people involved. Senator Morris. Trip Harrington. Patrick Derulo from QuinTech Missiles. In his inbox she got a few hits.

Trip Harrington especially. But as she skimmed each email, there was nothing suspicious. Trip wanted to handle finance for Zia. She searched again, her fingers a little too rough on the keyboard in her frustration. Nothing on the trust payouts either. She just had to keep digging. If there was nothing in this email, it was because he was too smart for that. He would be careful. Probably another personal account. What she really needed was his cell phone.

After an hour of fruitless searching in his inbox, Joey threw her hands up. She kicked her toe against the hard tile floor. She blew the hair out of her face and moved on to the task she had been assigned. Kensington had given her the specific protein injection codes she was looking for. Entering those into our search program pulled up mountains and mountains of data. A few names kept showing up on the documents. The team members no doubt. She wrote down their information so she could run background checks on all of them the next time she was at BTS. Surely, the ITS team at Zia had done that, but she was guaranteed to be more thorough. She found a few files that looked like summary reports of data. This is what she needed to duplicate with new fake results. With a brief glance, she copied the relevant documents. Most of it was nonsense gibberish to her.

She frowned at the realization that she was going to have to ask Kensington for help creating the fake reports. Great. As though she needed to spend more time with him.

To her left, she heard a beep, and the door opened. Her heart stopped. A security guard in a dark-blue uniform glared at her, then blinded her with a flashlight. She shielded her eyes instinctively.

"Who are you?"

———

After spending a few hours catching up and then going through the most recent data he had from the project, he sent a meeting invite to Laura, the head researcher on the CPB-PGI gene project, requesting a full update on the status. Cole ran his hands through his hair, tugging it in frustration. He'd dropped the ball, and there was nothing he hated more. He should have gotten this update before his meeting with the FDA, but he'd been distracted by the appearance of a certain cyber security specialist. He glanced at the empty space across his office that had been filled with boxes earlier. The stack of flat cardboard was still by the door. He couldn't remember the last time someone played a prank on him. Admittedly, he'd been amused

—at least slightly. But now he was just frustrated. He'd spent almost an hour dealing with that and his discussion with Joey afterward. When he should have been preparing for this meeting with the FDA. Even if it had been a super last-minute addition to his calendar for the week, it was no excuse.

He didn't know how he was going to put up with Joey long enough for her to finish what she'd been hired for. Or if he could resist trying to get to know her better.

He couldn't blame Joey entirely for his lack of preparation. Even if he'd spent the better part of the last several days either with her or thinking about her, it was his own fault. As much as he wanted to remain unaffected, he couldn't deny that Joey was a mystery he wanted to solve.

And it drove him crazy that she was able to get him to share things that he didn't typically share with anyone. He had almost told her about Jared, for crying out loud.

With more force than necessary, he logged out of his computer and shut it down. Time to call it a night. Or at least go have these circular thoughts from the comfort of his bed.

He texted Jared and flipped through his phone as he rode the elevator down to the lobby. When the elevator doors opened, he was greeted with the sight of one of his security guards. Cole's eyes widened. The guard had a woman, her arm pulled behind her back, and was forcing her down the hallway. She was struggling against him with little success. Seeing such force from his employee flooded him with horror in disbelief. What was going on?

"Let me go. I work here! This is all a big misunderstanding. Owww!"

Cole's blood ran cold as he recognized her voice.

Joey.

"Let her go. Immediately." It was bad enough that the guard was hurting anyone, let alone Joey.

The guard turned back. Joey stopped pulling, but the man didn't release her.

His voice hardened. "I said: Let. Her. Go!" He ground out each word through his tight jaw.

"Sir, she was in the server room without permission." The guard pulled her backward to straighten her stance, and a wince crossed Joey's face. The man was hurting her. Cole clenched his fists. He had to stop this, but how?

———

Joey's eyes watered with the increase in pain as the security guard tightened his hold, wrenching her arm behind her back. He was going to dislocate her shoulder, she was sure of it.

Cole stepped toward them. In a low, commanding voice, he spoke again. "Remove your hands or I will remove them for you."

Relief was immediate in her wrist and shoulder as the brute of a security guard finally let her go.

"You're dismissed," Cole's commanding tone came again. He'd used the same words with her earlier, and she'd thought them haughty and cold. It had been nothing compared to the iciness she heard in his voice right now as he spoke to the guard.

"But, sir," came the argument from the guard.

Cole held up a hand to silence the objection. "Go. Grab your things and get out of my building. Now. You're fired." She'd heard rumors around the office about Cole's hard demeanor and unforgiving standards. But since the first morning in the towncar, she hadn't seen much of it. He'd been a serious CEO, but the hard edge had been absent.

Until now.

"Cole," she said with a gentle warning. She shook her head. "I'm fine. It's okay. He was just doing his job."

His jaw clenched, and his palm came to her cheek, brushing away the wetness from the corner of her eye. "It's not okay," he said after he pulled it away.

He looked up at the guard. "You're on administrative leave. Effective immediately. I'll discuss this incident with Tommy, and we'll decide the appropriate discipline."

"Come on, man. She was in the server room. The system said there was no one in there. What am I supposed to think?" Joey winced. Her foolproof plan to spoof her access badge hadn't accounted for someone doing physical rounds and verifying the occupancy.

Cole raised his eyebrow and glanced at Joey. "Miss Rodriguez. Are you not an employee of the ITS department?"

She nodded. "I am."

"And is part of your job description performing server maintenance during off-peak hours?"

She nodded again, unsure what he was doing here.

"Does your clearance level grant you access to the server room?"

She nodded. "It does."

Cole opened his hands to his sides and looked back at the guard. "Then it sounds to me like we have a simple computer error, doesn't it, Mr. Elgin? Which certainly doesn't warrant dragging Miss Rodriguez around the building like some sort of criminal. I pay *you* to secure this building. I pay *her* to secure those computers. You're on the same team. You'd do well not to jump to conclusions next time and to treat people with respect. Got it?"

Joey rubbed her wrist as the security guard mumbled a weak apology, dropped her bag, and walked away.

Cole pulled her to the side of the hallway. His hands caressed her shoulders then her arms. Then the side of her head. He murmured quietly, "Are you okay? I'm so sorry, Joey."

"I'm fine, Cole. Seriously. It was all a misunderstanding. Don't fire him."

His lip twitched up, and she stared at it. Then she looked up at his eyes, which studied her with amusement.

"What did you say?" she asked. She'd missed something, her focus entirely on his half-smile for those few moments.

"I said, was it actually a misunderstanding? I'm assuming you're not here on official business? Which is why the log showed no record of your presence?"

She shrugged. "That is a distinct possibility." She

huffed. "I didn't realize the security rounds would include the server room. That's on me."

"Come on. Let's get you home. Do you have your car?"

She shook her head. "I took a cab. I was hoping the only person who would have any memory of me being here would be the front desk guard." She glanced down the hallway where the guard who'd found her in the server room had gone. "So much for that."

"It'll be okay. We'll write him up and suggest that telling anyone the details of the incident would find him looking for a new job instead of taking three days of unpaid vacation."

Joey chuckled, and they started moving toward the front door. "I'm glad you were here. I don't think Patrick would have appreciated the midnight wakeup call."

She felt his eyes on her and looked to find him staring. "I'm glad I was here, too. The way he was hurting you though…" His eyes darkened and his jaw tightened. "Are you sure I can't fire him?"

Joey stopped walking. "You really would, wouldn't you?"

She was trying to piece this information in with everything else she knew about Kensington. But the pieces didn't fit. Why would someone in the Syndicate care if she got hurt? She tried to read his tortured expression as he searched for words.

"I… I don't want you hurt," he said gruffly. "I know I hired you to do this job. But you can't get hurt on my account."

She grabbed his hand without thinking, which turned him toward her and brought him closer. She looked up at him, searching his face for any sign of deceit. He had to be playing her, right? But all she saw was concern. And weariness. His hair was tousled and his chin was covered with a dark shadow of stubble.

She squeezed his hand and released it so they could keep walking. "I'm not hurt. But are you okay? It's awfully late, and you seem… agitated."

He ran his hand through his hair, and Joey realized why it was so messy. "Yeah," he sighed. "Seeing that giant with his hands on you didn't help, but yeah. My nerves are pretty well shot tonight. Just a few complications with the project. We've got a deadline we didn't have before. Come on, I'll tell you about it on the ride home." They crossed the lobby and exited the front doors.

Jared stood by the car with the door open. His expression revealed nothing about his thoughts on

Joey getting into his boss's car at midnight, but Joey felt herself blush. "You remember where my house is, Jared?"

He nodded. "Yes, ma'am."

"Take the scenic route. We have a lot to discuss," Cole directed as Joey climbed in the car.

"My pleasure, sir."

# CHAPTER
## NINE

LATER THAT WEEK, Cole twisted his pen tightly as he listened to Laura Conwell. She stood across the executive conference room just outside his office. Her slides were well-organized, her presentation flawless.

But the information? That had him attempting to grind his poor ballpoint to dust.

"Give it to me straight, Laura. Are we back at square one?" He'd been working with Laura for two decades, since they did their graduate research together at Harvard.

Laura glanced back at her slides before responding. "Honestly, Cole? I don't know. I can't figure out what's happening. Sometimes I think I'm going crazy."

He frowned. He'd never heard Laura sound anything more than confident in her research conclusions. "What do you mean?"

"It's like…" She pressed a hand to her forehead and then waved it through the air in front of her. "Our vector trials were moving right along. Adenovirus vector 81B7 was showing really remarkable deliverability. But when we got to the final tally, it was less impressive than we thought."

"What about the sister vectors?"

She shook her head. "Same results. It's almost as if when I look at small pieces of data, everything makes perfect sense. And then as we aggregate the results, there are these anomalies. Results in the data that don't fit the pattern we expect. I know better than to trust the excitement we get during an individual test. Because the numbers don't lie in the end. I just wish I had better news to share. The CPB-PGI can't work if we don't pinpoint the right vector."

Or maybe they do. He glanced to his left, where his COO and CFO were sitting, taking in the update. "Can Laura and I have the room for a few moments?"

He gestured for his long-time friend to have a seat. He had to make a call about whether to trust her or not. Could he trust his gut? What would Joey do?

He stared at his pen. He knew exactly what she

would do. She'd dig into Laura's entire life and try to figure out if there was any way she was sabotaging the project.

"I know you wanted this to be the one, Cole."

"I want every single one to be the one, Laura. You know that." She knew that better than most people here. There was a lot of his job that required him to be detached and logical. To make decisions based on facts and figures rather than on emotions.

Usually, he was disciplined about it. He hated to let go of two hundred employees when he acquired a company and folded them into Zia. But the redundancy made it inevitable. It was business.

"We've been close before," he continued, "but I really thought this was it." He still thought this was it. But the data leak was going to ruin everything.

"Yeah. Me too. I'm sorry this didn't turn out better."

Cole took a deep breath. He wanted to trust her. For crying out loud, he'd been at her wedding. "I need five minutes to make a call. Wait here."

He ducked into his office and dialed Joey's extension.

"This is Joey," she answered. Her voice sent a ripple of awareness over him.

"Do you have a second?"

"Of course. How can I help?"

He narrowed his eyes at her helpful, professional tone. "Let me guess. People can hear you?"

"I *love* working in this open concept office. Privacy is overrated and computer work is so collaborative. No one down here complains about it at all."

He smirked at her obvious sarcasm. "Okay, I got it. I got it. Offices with real walls next time we renovate. I have a question. I'm thinking of looping in my lead researcher in my suspicions. I've known her since college. She's a good friend. But I figured I would make sure you have done your terrifying brand of wizardry to see if there are any red flags?" He nudged away the guilt that flared at the idea of digging into his friend's life. He was determined not to trust anyone though.

"What's the name?"

"Laura Conwell."

Joey's voice got quieter, and he strained to listen. "I remember the name. I didn't see anything in her personal life that raised major red flags. Some debt. But that's par for the course these days. Do you really need to bring her in though? I thought we had a plan? We could move forward and then bring her later. She's got the kind of access someone would need."

Cole ran a hand through his hair. "I hate this, Joey.

These are my people. I need to start clearing some names or I'm going to go insane."

"We'll work on it." Joey's voice brightened. "Thanks for checking in. I'll tell my father you said hello, Mr. Kensington."

His eyebrows flew upward. "I'll see you at BTS tonight."

He hung up without waiting for a response and went back to the conference room to a waiting Laura.

"Sorry about that."

"Is everything okay, Cole?"

He shook his head. "Not really. I can't share more right now, but I will soon. Can you send me the raw data files for this project?"

Her eyes were sympathetic. "Cole, you can't be serious. You don't have time to–"

He cut her off. "Just send them, Laura. I'll worry about my time."

Her objection silenced, Laura nodded curtly. "Yes, sir."

He sighed. "I'm sorry. I didn't mean to snap. I just–"

"I understand," she said. But he could hear the hurt in her voice.

Cole ground his teeth together. He hated everything about this. He paused for a moment, trying to convince himself to wait for Joey.

Then he shook his head sharply. "Oh forget it. She's not going to be happy, but whatever. I trust you. Come here," he insisted. "Here's the deal. I think someone is stealing our research in an attempt to derail our progress. And now, based on what you've shared here, I suspect it is someone internal and that not only are they stealing the research, but they are actively sabotaging the trials by tampering with the data."

Laura's horror was evident. If she was acting, she deserved an Oscar. "No, Cole. That's not possible. I know you're disappointed that the results aren't better, but no one on the team would–"

"Trust me, you think I like the idea that someone we trust is behind all of this? We're working to prove it, but I might need your help. For now, just act like everything is normal."

"We? Who is we? Who else knows about this?"

He shook his head. "I have someone from the outside helping. Our plan will work, especially with your help."

Laura was shaking her head. "I can't do this, Cole. How am I supposed to go back to the lab and face my team thinking that one of them is a traitor?"

"You have to. We don't have another option right now. It's just a few more days. Take a deep breath."

Laura did as instructed and he nodded. "Good. Okay. There's nothing to worry about right now, okay? Why don't you take the rest of the day off?" He was hoping that a few hours to let it sink in would help her composure.

She nodded. "I just can't believe it. Who would do such a thing?"

He stared blankly at the presentation still displaying on the large television across the room as Laura's words needled him. That was the very same question that plagued him at every turn.

———

Frustrated at Cole's assumption that he was invited, Joey considered not going to BTS headquarters after work at Zia. In the end, the allure of the equipment and her cave won out. If she needed to, she could just have Tank escort him out.

When he'd called her in the middle of the day, it had sent her day into a bit of a tailspin. Patrick had chosen that inconvenient moment to lean on the edge of her cubicle door. He must have eagle eyes because he'd spotted Kensington's name on her phone from across the space. Hopefully, her quick recovery had doused any suspicions.

Patrick didn't look especially impressed that the CEO was calling to check in on her first week. Perhaps it seemed a bit out of character. From what Joey had been able to gather, Kensington was all business, all the time. Most of her coworkers seemed equally intimidated and impressed by him. Only Patrick seemed unaffected. Was that simply because he worked more closely with the CEO? Or was it scorn or disrespect hidden by an overly casual demeanor?

Throughout the day, Joey created a list of things she needed to do once she was back at BTS. The system was simply too locked down at Zia for her to do things, like dig into the lives of people she came into contact with or decipher the maze of data she'd pulled off the server. And she still had to figure out who Cole was paying through the trust.

For that, she needed her arsenal of computers behind the secure network that would conceal her tracks. Which meant, once again, she was pulling into the parking lot of BTS long after most of the team had gone home. Not that business hours were much of a concept here. Depending on the job, it wasn't uncommon to work nights, weekends, or even a week straight traveling across the desert.

After skipping lunch to avoid passing the security office more than necessary lest she see her friend with the vise grips for hands, she'd been smart enough to grab herself dinner on the way. Unwrapping her sandwich, she settled into her computer gaming chair. She flipped on the built-in massage feature for good measure and sighed with relief, resting the sandwich on her lap as she shut her eyes for a moment. Maybe she should just start sleeping here.

"You look comfortable."

The voice made her jolt, and the sandwich toppled from her knees. She grabbed for it, fumbling for a grip on the paper. The sandwich landed with a splat on the floor below her feet. Joey stared at it for a moment, considering whether crying over a sandwich was reasonable.

She turned to glare at the interruption. "How did you even get in here?"

Cole shrugged and stepped inside, not waiting for an invitation. "Sorry to scare you. And about your sandwich."

She eyed him balefully.

He held up a paper bag. "Good thing I brought

dinner." He began to unpack the contents onto the corner of her desk.

She sniffed, and her mouth started to water at the scent of garlic. "Is that…"

"Napoli's," he confirmed.

She stared at the scattered remains of her drive-thru deli sandwich. "Sorry. You've been replaced."

She looked up to find Cole watching her with amusement.

"Were you just talking to the sandwich?"

"Just hand me a breadstick, big shot."

He quirked an eyebrow at her, but mercifully, a breadstick appeared in front of her. She snatched it from him and took a glorious bite. Closing her eyes, she let everything disappear except salt and garlic and butter and carbs.

The sound of Cole clearing his throat interrupted her momentary bliss. Jerk.

"Sorry," she said, embarrassed. "I didn't get a chance to eat lunch today."

He frowned. "Why not? Is Patrick overworking you?"

She shook her head. "No, nothing like that. It was my choice."

He pushed a container of food toward her. "You need to take care of yourself." Then he grabbed napkins and bent over to clean the mess off the floor. Her heart lurched at the sight of the billionaire CEO wiping lettuce and mayo off her chair mat.

"I'm fine. But thanks for this. I love Napoli's." The hole-in-the-wall Italian restaurant was a well-kept secret in Old Town Alexandria. She was surprised Kensington knew about it. "I would have pegged you as more of a Chez Celesti kind of guy." She looked up from her takeout just in time to see him shovel a fork loaded with noodles into his mouth.

His sheepish smile made her laugh as he grabbed a napkin and covered his mouth while he chewed. "Chez Celesti is fine. A little snooty if you ask me. Their sommelier is seriously the most pretentious guy. Plus, fifty bucks for a piece of lasagna? Come on. I'll take Nonna Ada's red sauce over a cloth napkin any day."

He dipped his breadstick into the sauce in the Styrofoam container and took a bite. She mirrored the action, letting this new tidbit sink into her mental dossier on him. He didn't seem to realize she needed time to process because, between bites, he looked at her computer.

"So what are we doing tonight?"

"I'm going to run that extra check on Laura for

you. Then I've got an algorithm I want to run on the data from the project."

"Oh. I should probably tell you that I already told Laura what was going on."

Joey paused her fork midway to her mouth. "You what?" Was the man insane?

Cole set his food on the desk. "Look, I needed to let her know. She cares just as much as I do. We've been working on this for decades together. I was at her wedding, for goodness' sake."

"I don't care if you're the godfather to her child. The fewer people who know what is going on, the easier it will be for us to find them." Joey set down her fork, her appetite disappearing in the rush of agitation.

"It's fine, Joey. I trust her."

"Yeah, well, I don't. And we're supposed to be a team here." She ignored the twinge of conscience at the clearly false declaration of unity. Just because she might buy his whole wanting to cure Alzheimer's bit didn't mean she wasn't pretty well-convinced that Kensington was doing some shady stuff to make it happen. Joey rolled her chair toward the desk. "If something comes up on her background check, you're the one who's going to have to confront her about it."

"Nothing will come up. And even if something

does… I'm sure it won't mean that she's behind all this. She would never."

Joey shook her head. "I love that you believe that." She hit a few buttons to get her deep dive program running, then turned back to Cole. "Look, I've been working in this world for a long time. If there is one thing I've learned, it's that people are capable of anything."

It was obvious that he would do anything to achieve his mission of curing Alzheimer's. And maybe that was part of the problem. Cole was so laser-focused on his mission that it seemed he had become capable of getting into bed with the worst of the worst.

She ran a hand through her hair. "When push comes to shove, people are only looking out for themselves. You might think they won't, but given the right incentive, everyone will betray you." It was a fact of life Joey had realized a long time ago.

"Who betrayed you, Joey?"

# CHAPTER
## TEN

THE QUESTION ESCAPED before he thought better of it.

Cole saw the intensity in Joey's eyes. She believed what she was saying with every fiber of her being. Everyone will betray you.

"Let's just say I would have sworn they never would. And yet, here we are."

"Is there anyone you trust without reservation?" Here was another layer to the Josephina onion. She wouldn't tell him who had betrayed her, but perhaps it was enough to know that someone had. His heart went out to her. He'd been let down by his parents. But betrayal? That was different.

Joey stared at the screen as it flipped through the

background check process she'd automated. "Without reservation? No."

"Not even Flint?" He had so many questions about their friendship. From what he could tell, if there was anyone she trusted, it was his friend.

She shook her head. "Not even Flint."

He lifted his eyebrows at her unexpected answer. Before he could ask for clarification, she continued. "This team? Black Tower comes close. I trust them with my life. I know they've got my back. Do I think they'd *want* to betray me? No. But do I think Flint would burn it all down if it meant saving Jessica?" She shrugged. "Probably. And that's how it should be."

Joey lifted her eyes to him. "Jessie's the most important thing in the entire world to him. You and I? We don't have that. Our most important thing isn't like theirs. It's not a person. It's a cause."

He let himself get lost in the dark-brown depths of her eyes. He could listen to her all night if she'd just keep talking.

"And what's your cause?" he asked quietly, urging her to continue.

She held his gaze and responded. "To save innocent people from those who would sacrifice them as pawns in a game they designed."

He didn't know what to make of that. It sounded incredibly noble. It also made him think there was a lot more happening at Black Tower than he realized. So much for security details and consultations. What had Flint gotten himself into?

What she'd said about him was true though. Nothing was more important to him than finding the cure. Stopping the disease. He was in a fight against nature.

A fight against the effects of a fallen world.

He supposed she was too. Stopping evil sounded like a tall order.

"Do you ever think you're fighting a losing battle?"

She exhaled a quiet laugh. "Yeah. Of course I do. There's too much crap in the world to think I could stop it all. But then again, don't you? How many researchers are devoting their life to fighting this terrible disease with nothing to show for it? Face it, Cole, if either of us makes a dent in the problems we face, we'll be fortunate."

"You can't think like that. If you've saved one person, if I've extended one memory for one extra day… It's made a difference."

"Maybe. The only thing that keeps me going is

knowing that I'm fighting a battle in a war that's already been won."

Cole paused, letting her words register. "How do you mean?"

Joey shrugged and grabbed her food again. "I do everything I can to fight for good and justice in this world. To take down the bad guys, right? But in the end, God already won. Evil, sickness, death, and sadness are all cast away when He returns."

"A lot of good that does when we're here right now," he responded bitterly. "Look, I love Jesus. But I'm not just going to sit on my heels and not try to help as people lose everything that made them who they are."

He had to make her understand how important this was. Did she really understand what was at stake? "Yes, it confuses their memories. But it can steal their personalities and rob them of the ability to take a walk without becoming combative or confused. And their family can't do anything but watch as the disease ravages their mind. It's awful, Joey."

Raw emotion burned his throat. How had they gotten here, with his heart torn open and poured out on the office floor in front of her? He pressed his eyes shut, afraid to see her reaction to his intense soliloquy.

"That's pretty much exactly how I feel about my fight. People use others and toss them aside. They kill, steal, lie. Whatever it takes to get what they want. And it makes me physically sick," she added. "Maybe we're not so different, Cole." He opened his eyes, and Joey leaned toward him in her chair, resting her elbows on her knees. "You've got skills that help you fight diseases. I've got skills that help me take down people that would use their power to marginalize the weak. God never told us to sit on our heels. We just can't lose perspective or we'd give up in the face of such daunting odds. God doesn't ask us to win the battle for him."

He exhaled a laugh. "Have you been talking to Flint?"

"Do you trust me to help you fight the evil that wants to stop you from fighting this disease?"

Cole lost himself for a moment in her intense stare. He swallowed thickly and nodded. "Yeah. I guess I do."

"Then be patient, and let us get there together. Don't bring in anyone else."

———

Joey poured a cup of coffee in the breakroom and listened to the conversation around her.

"When I was with Parsenix, we had an entire department that managed patient surveys. There were six of us, and we were a tenth of the size of Zia. I just don't know how we'll get this five-year patient questionnaire launched in the timeframe the executive team wants." Joey searched her brain for the woman's name. Cindy? Candi? Cheri, that was it.

"Seriously? What happened to all those folks from Parsenix?"

Cheri shook her head. "I was the only one who didn't get a pink slip when Zia bought us out. It was awful. I think of the three hundred of us, there are about ten of us still here."

"That's just like when we bought out Iris Bio. I heard a rumor that the only people Kensington kept on staff were from one specific research lab. Everyone else…" The man sliced his hand sideways in a cutting motion.

Joey turned her back to the conversation and hid her reaction to it until she could school her features. She replaced her disdain with curiosity and turned to face her coworkers. "Wow. Does that happen a lot around here?"

Cheri was happy to draw her into the conversation. "Oh yes. I swear everyone around here just managed to sneak through the cuts during one acquisition or another. Even Patrick. He's been here forever, but he was my manager at Parsenix. He took the buyout really hard. Especially after what happened to Michelle."

Joey's intrigue skyrocketed. "What happened to Michelle?"

Cheri's original conversation partner dumped his cup and waved as he ducked out of the breakroom.

Cheri leaned in after looking around to make sure no one else could hear. "She was another woman in our department. She didn't make the cut. She ended up getting a divorce and losing her house. We found out six months after the buyout that she killed herself."

"Oh my goodness, that's awful."

Cheri nodded. "I know. Patrick took it really hard. Blamed himself."

"Why would he blame himself?"

She shrugged. "I heard Kensington made him select the people to keep around."

"Ooh, yikes." No manager wanted to be put in that situation. At least Patrick seemed to have moved on. Other than his irritation that Cole had brought Joey into the group without his input,

Patrick only spoke with admiration, as far as Joey could tell.

Ben shuffled into the breakroom. Joey and Cheri exchanged a look as he got a soda from the vending machine before shuffling back out. As he reached the door, he grumbled at Joey. "Your phone keeps ringing. I unplugged it."

Beside her, Cheri choked on her coffee.

Joey opened her mouth to respond to Ben's ridiculous rudeness, but he was already gone.

"Wow," she said instead.

"You're Joey, right?" Cheri leaned back against the counter, kicking one heel over the other.

Joey smiled broadly and held out her hand. "Oh, sorry. Yeah, I'm Joey. I've only been here two weeks or so. It still feels like I have so much to learn."

Cheri laughed. "Well, don't let Ben get under your skin. He's like that with everyone."

She shook her head. "I've worked with some pretty eccentric computer guys over the years. Rarely are they quite that bad."

With a wave of her cup, she said good-bye to Cheri. "I guess I better go plug my phone back in. It was nice chatting with you."

"You too. Good luck, Joey."

Back at her desk, Joey flipped through her caller

ID and saw that Ryder had called her twice. Curious, she called him back, speaking in low tones from her cubicle.

"Hey, I saw you called."

"Can you talk?"

"Sort of."

"Roger that. I wanted to let you know as soon as I found out. But you know that blind trust you asked me to look into? It turns out that Kensington is the only contributor. And the beneficiary? The Honorable Theresa Martin, a judge in the 4th Circuit.

"What?!"

Joey felt the eyes turn to her with the exclamation. She smiled and then ducked her head. "Are you sure, Ryder?"

"Oh, I'm sure. It wasn't easy, but I went to Salem and asked around. Apparently, Judge Martin's husband has been disabled and in full-time care for nearly twenty-five years."

Joey raised her eyebrows. That would make her an easy target for bribery. Those kinds of expenses weren't exactly easy to cover. And twenty-five years? A federal judge made good money, but at the start of her career, she was probably just like any other struggling caretaker.

"Do we have any idea why he's bribing a federal judge?"

"I'm still working on it," Ryder said.

"Okay. Keep digging." This was a big break. Something like this, even Flint couldn't deny.

"Hey, Jo?"

"Yeah?"

"Watch your back."

"I will," she reassured him quietly before disconnecting the phone.

"Who was that?"

The gruff voice caused her to turn and look up at Ben, who was standing in his cubicle, peering into hers.

"Oh, umm… It was just a friend."

Ben rolled his eyes. "Try to take your personal calls on your personal time."

After he sat down, Joey mouthed a sassy mimicry of his words. She couldn't help but wonder if he'd heard anything though. The majority of the call, she'd simply been listening to Ryder, but she didn't like that Ben had been listening. Where were his stupid headphones today?

Last night at Black Tower, she'd worked through some of the test data from Kensington's CPB project. There were some things that didn't add up, so her plan tonight was to verify the data on the equipment in the lab. She knew that just because the data on the server looked one way, it didn't mean that the actual original test results were the same.

She'd spend some time in the lab, matching the data on the reports to the data on the machine. Thankfully, the records were very thorough and she'd be able to pinpoint equipment and results very quickly. She didn't have to know what numbers meant in order to validate the data.

This would help them narrow down if the process was happening before the reports were generated or after they were on the server.

"Joey, can you come in here?" The request came from the door of a conference room on the edge of the open-concept office area. "We're talking through updates to our internal firewall before the next vulnerability scan."

She tipped back her coffee, gearing up for another late night.

# CHAPTER ELEVEN

COLE CHECKED HIS WATCH. "Janet, you might as well go home. I'll be here for a while, but there's no need for you to miss dinner."

"Are you sure, Mr. Kensington? Do you want me to order you some dinner?"

"No thanks." He'd just grab a granola bar and try to leave right after he met with Laura. Her email earlier had been cryptic, but hopefully she would clear things up when they talked later. He had an hour and a half before he was due to meet her in the genetics lab on 2B. The basement laboratories of Zia were some of the most advanced labs in the country, with equipment he'd only dreamed about as a grad student twenty-five years ago.

Some days, he wished he could spend his time

down there, running the tests and compiling the data. Instead, he was layers away. Any results he saw had been summarized and organized and sanitized for executive consideration. But he was a scientist at heart.

Still, even though he had the research background, he'd quickly recognized that others were far superior to him in intellect and analytical skills. He had something many of the technical staff didn't: the ability to manage people and strategize the big-picture ideas. Setting aside his lab coat nearly fifteen years ago, he now trusted his employees to take care of the detailed work of research, development, and clinical trials.

When his calendar alert pulled him away from the financial reports he was reviewing at a quarter-to-seven, Cole grabbed his coat, wallet, and phone and got in the elevator. He swiped his access badge before punching the 2B button.

The elevator doors opened a few moments later, and Cole stepped out. The lab was quiet. It was Friday night, so he wasn't surprised the research teams were gone. It was probably why Laura had invited him to meet at this time. When he worked in the lab himself, he'd realized quickly that more hours didn't always mean more output. Instead, he encouraged his teams to plan their experiments so that lengthy processes ran overnight and to make sure they were well-rested. He'd rather wait an extra week than risk a mistake made due to researcher fatigue.

Through one more set of access-restricted double doors, the CPB lab spread out before him. Low-walled cubicles were scattered throughout the open room, with counters surrounding the edges sporting microscopes and centrifuges below shelves stacked with glassware and safety equipment. The surfaces gleamed, filling Cole with a sense of pride and satisfaction.

There was no sign of Laura, so he moved toward her office, a small private room to the right of the main door. Other rooms branched off the main workspace, smaller labs for specialized equipment, animal testing, and specimen storage. The light was on, but the door was cracked, so he knocked lightly. "Hey, I–"

His voice cut off in a strangled cry as he saw the splatter of crimson on the wall, his eyes then dropping to the pool of blood on the floor, the edges just visible from his position in front of the desk. Rushing forward, he found her. "Laura!" He pressed a hand to her neck, desperately hoping to feel a pulse. There was so much blood. Cool and sticky, it covered his hands as he searched for a sign of life.

"No, no, no. Laura!" He looked around helplessly. It was as if his brain wouldn't work. He didn't know what to do. He just stared at his friend.

"Cole?"

He whipped his head toward the door and saw Joey, her eyes wide with horror.

"Cole, what happened? What did you do?" She was backing away, hands up in front of her. Her eyes flicked down to Laura and then back to him.

He flinched at the accusation. "What? No. Laura. She's been shot or…" He shook his head, desperately trying to comprehend what to do. "There's so much blood, Joey. It's her neck. What do I do?"

A door slammed out in the lab, and Joey's head jerked toward the sound.

"Call 911!" she yelled before disappearing out of the office, leaving him with the body of his friend. He glanced down at Laura, recognizing for the first time the reality that Laura was already gone.

An ambulance wouldn't do any good.

———

Joey ran toward the noise, bursting into the stairwell. No sign of anyone. She jogged up two flights of stairs, startled when footsteps pounded behind her. She glanced back and saw Cole chasing her.

Her heart accelerated. So this was where she would die—after witnessing a murder by a billionaire CEO. He probably had people who would clean the whole scene and no one would ever find her body.

Her legs and lungs burned with the effort of running from him.

She reached the lobby floor, her heart pumping wildly as she gasped for air. She glanced back at Cole, steps behind her. She backed away from him, stumbling toward the next set of ascending stairs. "Please don't–"

He pointed to the emergency exit. "They must have gone out the side door," he said through his ragged breath as he came to a stop on the landing.

Her thoughts were scattered and fragmented, but she paused her retreat. He wasn't coming after her?

She scolded herself for being so ridiculous. Of course, Cole wasn't trying to kill her. It was all in her imagination, fueled by adrenaline and the sight of a dead body with Kensington leaning over it.

First of all, they'd heard someone leaving the basement. And second of all, what was the likelihood that a billionaire was doing his own dirty work?

No, there was someone else. Someone who had, in fact, shot the woman downstairs.

Her gaze followed Cole's gesture, and she became aware of the high-pitched ringing from the emergency exit alarm on the door beside them. Joey pushed the door open and was greeted with an unfamiliar alley. She took a few steps out, jogging toward the street, where the silhouette of a man was nearing the end of the alley.

A flash of light and a loud bang made Joey duck.

A gun!

She scrambled to the edge of the alley, searching for cover. Another shot fired, and pieces of brick rained down on her as the bullet struck the building overhead.

Cole yelled at her from the doorway. "Get in here!" She flinched at another gunshot and darted toward Cole.

She ducked behind the door, waiting for more gunfire.

"We have to go after him," she urged.

"Are you crazy? The man has a gun. He killed Laura. Besides, he's long gone by now," Cole replied.

Dang it.

Kensington was right.

With one last careful glance at the now empty

alley through the cracked door, they went back to the basement. Cole went ahead of her, and when Joey came back to the office door, Cole was next to the body, holding Laura's hand and staring intently at it. Her gaze faltered on his normally perfect suit covered in dark-red stains. His hands, sticky with blood. "Cole." She tried to get his attention. He didn't look at her. "Cole," she tried again, louder this time.

Undoubtedly, this sight of Cole covered in blood would haunt her.

"Cole!" she finally yelled. He jolted and looked her way.

"She's dead," he said, his voice strangely detached from emotion now that the intensity of the previous moments had passed.

She softened her voice. "Cole, you need to get out of the office."

He looked around, as though seeing the space for the first time. "Who would have done this?"

Joey shook her head. "I don't know. I do know that they're probably going to assume you did. We need to call some backup. Do you have a lawyer?"

Cole blinked and looked back at Laura. Joey saw his pain clearly reflected in his face. How could she have thought he had done this? "Come on," she said again. "Let's get you into the other room. Call security. They're going to need tapes. Access logs. Everything."

As the 911 dispatcher asked him questions, he looked up at her, and Joey's heart broke at the anguish on his face. How had he ever seemed cold to her? Now, as tears streamed down his face, it seemed impossible she had ever thought that. He shook his head.

"No," he choked out in response to something on the line. He hit a button to put the call on speaker phone.

"The police are coming. Please don't touch anything, sir. It is a crime scene."

Joey waited until the call disconnected. "Cole. Did you see anything when you got here? Anything at all?"

He shook his head and reached to run his hands through his hair. She was coming to realize he did it when he was stressed. Even more so after business hours were over. He stopped as his hands came in front of his face. He grimaced and shut his eyes. "No. Nothing. It was quiet. I was supposed to meet Laura at seven to talk about the project. To talk about our suspicions." He eyed Joey. "What are you doing here? You don't have lab access."

Yikes. He was right. She hated to physically

doctor the access logs, knowing that the police would need them in their investigation. But those logs weren't going to show her arrival, which would be suspicious.

"My algorithm found some anomalies in the vector efficacy dataset. Data points that seem to be altered to appear as random poor results. But they aren't random enough."

He frowned. "Not random enough. What does that even mean?"

"A person trying to create randomness will almost always create a pattern that only *seems* random. True randomness is hard to fake. I was going to compare the data on the server to the raw data on the equipment hard drive."

"Oh."

She grimaced. "But we do have a problem. You're right. Technically, I'm not supposed to be down here. And the access logs don't show any trace of me. So…"

"You came in with me then," he stated firmly.

She shook her head. "The elevator camera will debunk that pretty quickly." She paused. "But maybe it can tell us who killed Laura. Are there more cameras down here?"

"Just at the entrance." Cole grabbed the phone and

dialed security. Joey quickly pulled up to the closest computer and accessed the security server information. She glanced at the door every few minutes, sure the police were going to barge in any minute and arrest both of them.

She found her ghost access record and updated it to show her normal access badge, adding a temporary authorization for B2 to her ITS badge access permissions. "If anyone asks, I was invited to this meeting you had with Laura, got it?"

Cole looked up from the phone. "Of course. Seven o'clock."

She smiled tightly, grateful he was willing to go with it. "And you authorized a temporary access for my badge."

He raised an eyebrow. "How else could I invite you to a meeting down here?" He paused and held her gaze. "It's going to be okay," he said with a solemn look.

She nodded, strangely comforted by his words. Despite everything—all her prejudices and suspicions—she believed him.

Someone must have answered the phone because he turned slightly and began speaking. The cool, detached CEO she knew was back. Yet again, Joey wrestled with the idea of who the real Cole Kensington was. The man in tears over his friend? Or the man sending bribes to a federal judge? The one ruthlessly firing two-hundred people to earn an extra buck?

"Tommy, I'm glad you answered. We've got a major situation. I need you to get back here now." He paused, then continued. "I know, and I wouldn't ask if it wasn't important. Laura's been murdered, Tommy. In the lab."

# CHAPTER
# TWELVE

COLE WATCHED as the crime scene techs dropped his Brioni suit into an evidence bag. He now sported a spare T-shirt and shorts from Tommy's gym locker.

"Walk me through what happened again," the detective instructed. "You came out of the elevator and…"

Cole sighed. This was at least the fourth time he'd recounted the evening's events. The detective asked a few questions, ones Cole was certain he'd already mentioned.

"And this other woman…" The detective looked at his notes. "Josephina?"

Cole nodded. "We had a meeting with Laura scheduled at seven. Joey arrived a few minutes after I did. We heard a door close. I'm pretty sure it was the stairwell. We both took off after whoever it was. When we got up to the ground floor, he shot at us in the alley before we came back inside."

"And you have no idea why someone would kill Ms. Conwell?" The detective's question was laced with skepticism and assumptions.

Cole searched the room until they landed on Joey. She sat at one of the desks on the far side, away from Laura's office, another officer questioning her.

"No, I don't. Everyone loved Laura. She's been the director of this lab for fifteen years."

"Were the two of you romantically involved?"

Cole reared back. "What? No. Laura was my friend and employee. That is all. She loved her husband!"

"That must have made you angry? Her devotion to another man?"

He struggled to maintain his composure. "This is ridiculous. How many times do I have to tell you, there was nothing between Laura and myself? Look, Officer—"

"Detective," the man corrected him.

Cole pressed his lips together in frustration. "My apologies. Detective," he conceded. "It's awfully late. My security team will get you whatever you need as far as camera footage and security logs. But it's been a long day, and Laura was a very close friend. And I'd like to leave now."

The detective appeared especially smug as he closed his notebook. "Sure, Mr. Kensington. Are you willing to come down to the precinct if we have any further questions?"

He resisted the urge to groan. "Of course," he agreed politely. Then, with a flat expression, he added, "You can reach out to my lawyer to arrange it." Cole wrote down the name and number of his attorney. "Though I can't think of anything I haven't already told you."

Well, other than the whole potential motive regarding the gene therapy trials. And the fact that it was Cole who'd put her in danger by telling her about someone sabotaging the trials.

The detective grimaced but accepted the card. "Well, sometimes people *remember* things later. After the fact, you know?"

Cole could already tell he was the prime suspect. But they hadn't arrested him, so that was a good start.

"Am I free to go?" he asked.

The detective nodded. "Yes, sir."

Cole approached the desk where Joey sat. "Are you ready to go?"

The detective looked up with irritation. "I'm still asking Ms. Rodriguez a few more questions."

Joey straightened. "I've already told you everything I saw, heard, felt, and smelled."

"Sounds like you've got what you need. I'll be taking Ms. Rodriguez home now," Cole said, using his boardroom voice. It left no room for arguments. "You can contact her lawyer if you have additional questions. Your partner over there has the details." It was an easy decision. Her lawyer would be his lawyer, because he was going to make sure she had the very best that money could buy.

Joey frowned at him, but thankfully, didn't argue.

He walked silently beside her to the elevator, barefoot, since his shoes had been seized as evidence also. Joey reached over and pushed the call button, then stepped back, a little closer to his side.

Neither of them said anything as they stepped into the elevator and waited for the doors to close. He desperately wanted to wrap his arm around her. He glanced at the camera he knew was hidden in the corner of the ceiling.

He teased her fingers with his, finding two of them and squeezing gently.

Her grip tightened in response, forging a secret link between them, hidden by the long sleeves of her coat. He clenched his jaw, holding back the emotion behind a pressure valve that he couldn't afford to let burst. Not yet.

An unspoken bond had been built between them tonight. He held Joey's fingers tightly, releasing only as the elevator doors opened. She pointed toward the parking garage and met his eyes. He shook his head. He couldn't explain it, but he wanted her with him.

"No way you're driving home tonight. Come on." He nodded toward the front door where his car would be waiting. Her eyes fluttered shut before she nodded.

"Okay," she said quietly. They crossed the quiet lobby, the gleaming surfaces reflecting the dim lights, and headed out to the car. Joey looked at him after seeing the driver. It wasn't Jared. Cole nodded in response, a wordless conversation taking place. It was okay. When Jared was off, he used a car service he trusted.

He leaned down to whisper in her ear. "Jared gets a night off every now and then."

Joey stopped and looked up. "Do you know him? Because you nearly witnessed a murder downstairs… and there is no way we're getting in a car with a driver you've never seen before."

Cole was torn between a frustration born mostly of fatigue and a begrudging respect that Joey wouldn't let her guard down, even after everything they'd been through already. She had to be as worn down as he was.

"This is Tyler. He's been driving for me as needed for about three years, right, Tyler?"

"Yes, sir, about that."

"How's your daughter? Still at Ball State?"

Tyler's smile came easily at the mention of his daughter. "Yes, sir. She graduates in May with her degree in business marketing."

Joey had relaxed next to him. Cole ushered her inside the vehicle while responding to the proud father. "Congratulations. Send me her resume. We can always use good marketing folks."

"I will do that. Thank you, sir."

After telling Tyler where they were headed, Cole settled in next to Joey. Because he needed it, and because he thought she might need it too, he held open his arm, inviting her to sit closer. She glanced at the open space for a moment before sliding across the leather and sinking under his arm, against his body. He wrapped his arm around her and let himself shut his eyes.

Almost immediately, he opened them again, willing the scene from earlier to stop replaying in his mind. Joey shifted so she could look at him.

"Are you okay?"

He shook his head. "No. Not really. Are you?"

"Not even a little. I think we underestimated the threat here, Cole."

He'd been thinking the same thing. Talking with the police, he hadn't disclosed much about the research, but whoever had killed Laura knew intimate details about the project and either worked at Zia or was able to gain access.

He laid his head back and stared at the ceiling of the car. "Someone killed her, Joey. This is my fault, isn't it?" He felt Joey shake her head. "I brought her into this mess by telling her I suspected something was wrong. She must have confronted someone or mentioned my concerns to the wrong person. What about her husband? Her kids?" He pressed his eyes shut against the sting of tears.

Joey sat up. He missed the warm pressure of her leaning on him. Reluctantly, he opened his eyes and tipped his head up.

She looked at him quietly for a moment, and he wondered what she saw. He was in basketball shorts and a T-shirt that didn't belong to him. He felt like Laura's blood would never come off his hands, despite his best attempts using the commercial-grade cleanser in the lab.

"You didn't kill her, Cole. Whoever we chased up the stairs and was in that basement? They killed her. And the police and your security team and Black Tower? We'll figure out who it was and we'll make sure they face justice. Okay?"

She was so determined, so strong in her declaration that Cole didn't have another option besides nodding his agreement. He realized that, until now, he had trusted Flint—and Joey by extension—with his company. Now, it would seem he was going to have to trust her with his life. Just as easily as this person had killed Laura, they could come after him as well. He had no idea what Laura had said before she died. Did the killer know that Cole was suspicious? If so, he was a target.

At least Joey was still safe. Unless the killer had somehow seen her in the lab tonight, her cover should still be intact. That was a relief, though tempered a bit by the reality that the police still likely had her in their sights.

The last thing he wanted to do was get her hurt. As much as she challenged him and as much as her snarky attitude irritated him at times, thinking about Joey in danger because of him was unacceptable. He'd already caused the death of one woman he cared about.

Not that he cared about Joey, per se. That wouldn't be appropriate. He was her boss.

Kind of.

Oh, who was he kidding? As much as he didn't want to, he couldn't deny he cared about her. Even if he still didn't really know if she even liked him, Joey had gotten under his skin. She was unlike any woman he'd ever met.

He didn't want her hurt. "We're calling Flint," he said suddenly.

Her eyes widened. "Right now?"

He glanced at his watch, then grimaced at the empty spot on his wrist. It had been seized as evidence as well. "What time is it, Tyler?"

"It is a quarter after midnight, sir."

He blew out a breath. It might as well be three in the morning with how tired he was. "I'll send him a message, and we'll talk first thing in the morning."

# CHAPTER THIRTEEN

JOEY WATCHED the streetlights roll by without paying much attention. The adrenaline from the encounter this evening had faded, and she was near to falling asleep with her head on Cole Kensington's shoulder. The thought brought a small smile to her lips.

When he'd opened his arm so she could sit next to him, she'd briefly considered refusing. But after the second longest day in her life, her willpower was completely nonexistent. Sometimes, you just needed physical contact. A tactile reminder that you were still alive and your heart was still beating

She would have leaned into just about anyone in that moment. Tank, Ryder, even Jackson who rubbed her the wrong way at nearly every turn.

It was a nice gesture for Cole to offer. That's all.

He felt solid and strong against her side, and she let her eyes close. When they opened again, she realized the car had stopped. She leaned up and glanced out the window. They were in a garage. Her heart raced. "Cole?" She looked at him; his eyes were closed. "Cole!" She shook him awake.

"Hmm?" His groggy hum irritated her. Couldn't he see they'd been taken?

"Where are we? Where did you take us?" she yelled the accusation at the driver.

Cole shifted in his seat and reached for her hand. "Shh, it's okay, Joey. We're just at my house."

She leaned away, fighting against the seatbelt. "Say what now?" Her panic was quickly fading into irritation and anger.

"Relax, Joey. Don't fight me. I don't have the energy right now."

"Well, you better find the energy, Mr. Kensington. Because there is no way I'm staying at your house."

Cole rolled his eyes. "You are. Because I need you somewhere safe until we figure out what's going on. And because we have an 8 AM meeting with Flint right here."

Joey opened her mouth to object again. Then

closed it. She inhaled, planning her rebuttal. Then sagged.

"Fine. But just for tonight."

"We'll see," was Cole's response. She felt a bit like a five-year-old being placated for the moment to think he'd get what he wanted later. If Cole wanted to defer the disagreement to later, she was fine with that.

It seemed only a few minutes later that Joey woke up, surrounded by the luxuriously decadent guest bed. She hadn't spent a lot of time studying her surroundings as Cole led her to the guest suite, but through the lens of her weariness, the home seemed surprisingly modest, not to mention inviting and cozy. Cole had no right being soft and inviting. She needed him to be detached, cool, and untouchable. She'd expected a cold, modern penthouse with stark lines and impractical furniture designed to be art, valuing form over function.

But this bed was definitely hitting function on the nose. She hadn't slept that well in years. The sun was just beginning to creep through the window behind gauzy curtains. She stretched, groaning as her muscles protested the movement.

Cole was the most prepared host she'd ever seen, and she slipped a robe over the pajamas that Cole had pulled from the guest closet last night. It made staying here seem more like a vacation than an emergency. In the past, crashing at a friend's house meant sleeping in her jeans on a futon in the living room.

Here, it was a thousand thread count sheets, silk pajamas, and a cotton robe. Getting too used to this would be dangerous.

She tiptoed out of the guest suite and down the stairs toward her vague recollection of the kitchen. Coffee sounded heavenly. What she found when she entered the kitchen made her steps falter along with her heartbeat.

Cole Kensington, one of the most influential men in the country with a bank account that rivaled that of a small kingdom and topped every list of eligible bachelors. That Cole Kensington? He was in flannel pajama pants, slippers, and a deliciously fitted white T-shirt. His hair was rumpled, and he wore black-framed glasses she'd never seen before in any picture. And he was cracking an egg into a pan.

Her hand found her necklace. Oh, what a sight.

She cleared her throat and continued down the steps, determined to pretend she was unaffected.

He glanced up and smiled. "Good morning," he said. "Would you like some coffee?"

"Is social media a giant grab for personal information by evil corporations?"

He blinked in response and shook his head. "What?"

Joey chuckled and translated her response. "Yes. I'd love some coffee."

"Right."

She took a seat at the bar across the counter from the stove and pretended not to watch as he reached for a mug from an upper cabinet, his muscles shifting under his shirt. He filled it and set it in front of her, then slid a bowl with sugar and a carton of cream. Joey wasn't sure why she was surprised that it was the same brand of half-and-half she had in her own fridge. What did she expect? It wasn't as if billionaires had to import every ingredient just because they could.

She put her nose over the mug and inhaled deeply before taking a sip. She nearly moaned in appreciation as the smooth, rich flavor hit her tongue. He might not go the extra mile for the cream, but the coffee? It was top-notch.

Joey turned her gaze back to Cole.

"What would you like in your omelet?"

She looked at the bowls of ingredients. "No mushrooms, please. Everything else sounds good though."

He sprinkled the rest of the ingredients onto the

smooth layer of cooking eggs. "I'm impressed," she said.

"Don't be too impressed. I usually fumble the flip and then end up making a scramble instead of an omelet."

She chuckled. "Either way, it tastes the same. This is way more than necessary."

He flipped one half of the omelet over, no fumbling at all.

"Do I lose points if I admit that my housekeeper preps everything I need?" He slid the omelet onto a plate, added a piece of toast, and placed it in front of her.

"Not even a little," she admitted.

"Oh, good," he replied with a wink as he cracked another egg in the pan.

Before Joey could wonder too much why Cole would be concerned about earning and keeping points from her, the door opened behind her. Instead of turning around, she watched Cole's body language. He smiled.

"Morning, Cole," she heard, recognizing Flint's voice.

Joey turned so Flint could see her. "Hey, boss."

"Joey. Are you okay?" Flint's concern warmed her as much as the coffee. What had started as Flint's divine interference in her FBI arrest had turned into a friendship she'd never take for granted.

"I'm okay." She gestured to Cole with a nod. "He's the one who found her. And lost his friend," she added sadly.

She looked back at Cole and found him running a hand through his hair. He'd clearly taken the worst of the damage yesterday, and yet here he was, taking care of her with breakfast and a place to stay.

She looked back at Flint. There was something in her friend and mentor's expression that made her pause. "What aren't you telling me?"

Flint sighed. "Miranda sent Connor to grab your car from Zia this morning."

That was Miranda, always taking care of the details for the team. "And?"

"The tires had been slashed."

Her mouth fell open.

Cole straightened, an angry scowl on his face. "Seriously?"

Flint nodded. "I'm afraid so. I'd like to look at the security tapes. We can't be sure yet if it was before or after the murder."

Joey stabbed a piece of egg with her fork. "Worst-case scenario?" she asked Flint.

He hesitated. "Worst-case scenario is that it was

the killer and it was done after the incident in the alley. Maybe laying a trap so he could get to you while you were stranded in the garage."

She sagged. That was definitely not a rosy picture. If Cole hadn't insisted on giving her a ride last night… She glanced at him to find his eyes on hers. Apparently, the same thoughts were rolling through his mind.

"Well, this sucks," she said.

Cole choked on his coffee. "Joey!" his exasperated cry made her laugh.

She shrugged her shoulders and threw her hands up. "What? It does suck. In all likelihood, the killer saw me in the alley, or at the very least saw my car in the garage, and figured the person who owned it was the one person who can tie him to the murder."

Cole sighed. "I know. You're right. I hate everything about this. Our number-one priority is to keep you safe." He ran a hand through his hair. "Honestly, I'm tempted to shut down the entire project."

She sucked in a sharp breath. "You can't do that, Cole. You're so close."

He rested his elbows on the counter and cradled his head in his hands as they fisted in his hair. "I know. But no one was ever supposed to die." He tipped his chin up, his eyes zeroing in on hers, laced with sadness. "I'm supposed to save lives, right?"

Joey's heart squeezed with sorrow for his tortured plea. Before she could follow her foolish desire to step around the counter and soothe his worry with a touch, Flint spoke again.

"Maybe we should call it off, Cole. At least until the police have a chance to catch the guy."

Joey tensed at Flint's recommendation. "No way," she argued. "The police are convinced Cole is the shooter anyway. The best thing we can do is continue with our plan. We find the mole and we find the killer."

There was no way she was going to hole up waiting for this to blow over. Not when she could be helping.

She pressed her lips together, waiting for Flint to make the call.

"All right, Joey. You might be right. I don't think our killer is going to do anything in broad daylight at work. I'm sending in Tank and Will with you."

Joey started to object. "That's really not—"

"Is that enough?" Cole asked.

Joey looked at him in surprise. Cole had been so hesitant to let her inside his pharmaceutical fortress, she'd expected him to put his foot down about more BTS staff.

Flint responded to Cole's question. "It should be. They'll look out for Joey and help see the mission through."

"I don't need a babysitter, Raven," she insisted. Tank wasn't exactly inconspicuous anywhere he went. And Will Gilbert was one of the best operatives she'd ever seen. And he was Ross McClain's right-hand man. Ross was the co-owner of Black Tower along with Flint.

Usually, Will was sent out on a lot of solo missions. Even she didn't know many of the assignments he was given. They were classified even within the team. That was some serious backup Flint wanted to throw at this.

"I think it's a good idea," Cole said. His gaze nearly burned a hole in her when he continued. "I won't let anything happen to you." Joey started to shake her head to disagree, but Cole leaned closer. "Joey, whoever the killer is, he saw you in the alley. Possibly slashed your tires. And if there's any chance you can identify him, I'm guessing he's not going to let you go. You have to trust us."

Joey swallowed her objections. Trusting Flint she could do. And Tank and Will. But trusting Cole? That would be harder. Even after last night, there were so many unanswered questions. He might not be a killer. And he had been surprisingly thoughtful with her and concerned about her safety.

But he had also destroyed lives through his business tactics, had a convicted felon as his right-hand man, was apparently paying off a judge, and still had far too many connections to Syndicate members. Part of her was desperate to trust him. And the other was frantically trying to fit the pieces of the puzzle together in a way that made sense.

After a moment, she nodded. "Okay, fine. Will and Tank can come to the party."

"Joey, this isn't a joke," Cole said. His eyes were serious, concerned.

"I know that. But honestly, if I don't laugh, I'm afraid I'll cry. And I hate to cry. I just want to figure out who this is so it can all be behind us."

"Where are you at with the false report?" Flint's quiet question shifted the direction of the conversation. She was grateful for the redirect because if they spent any more time talking about how her life was in danger, she was likely to scream.

Joey straightened. "I've got the groundwork laid. I need someone to help make it a convincing fake. Cole, I guess that's you?"

He nodded. "Sure."

"Have you heard anything from the police?" she asked him. Maybe they'd caught the culprit. It would sure make walking into the office on Monday a lot easier.

Cole shook his head. "Nothing yet. Tommy said the videos didn't show a face. The detective didn't seem too concerned about the other person anyway. And access logs show that the only person in the lab was Laura, until I showed up."

She frowned. "How can that be?"

Cole sagged. "I don't know. Apparently, my security system needs an upgrade."

Joey shook her head. "I don't think so. I want to look at the logs again. Maybe I missed something?"

"You never miss anything, Joey," Flint replied confidently.

"Even so… I have to do something. Point me to a computer."

Flint replied, "The best thing you can do is finish up that fake report so our mole sticks his head up again."

"And then?" Cole asked.

Flint smacked his hand on the counter. "Whack-a-mole, obviously."

Joey chuckled, then glanced at Cole with concern.

As part of BTS, she knew that sometimes humor was the only way to get through a serious situation. But how would Cole react to a joke like that, when it was his company and life goal on the line?

He didn't laugh, but he smiled slightly at Flint. "Thanks, man." He turned to Joey. "You can use my office. If you need anything else, we'll have it brought over from BTS. You're staying here for a few more days."

Joey choked on her coffee. Flint raised his eyebrows before responding. "We can keep her safe at BTS, Cole. Or Miranda can get her a safehouse."

Joey struggled to breathe as their exchange continued. Cole wanted her to stay here?

Cole nodded. "I'm sure you can. But here, we can work on the report. And my beds are more comfortable."

Joey pointed a playful finger at Cole's excuses. "He's not wrong. That bed should come with a warning label. May cause inability to sleep anywhere else ever again." Even Miranda's legendary ability to find last-minute accommodations couldn't compete with that bed. "But I'll stay at BTS," she said firmly, ignoring Cole's pained expression.

It was sweet he wanted to protect her. But also, she worked at a security firm that employed a handful of ex-military commandos and had the most high-tech security system in the world. Cole might not like to concede, but he had to admit she would be fine.

She finished her omelet and took the plate to the sink. She came back for her coffee cup and found Cole already topping it off. "Thanks," she said.

"Come on, I'll show you the office."

Flint waved a hand. "I'll wait here. Then you and I can talk about how to get Tank and Will established inside Zia with Joey."

# CHAPTER FOURTEEN

COLE CARRIED his coffee in one hand as he led Joey back up the stairs. He couldn't remember the last time he'd had someone stay at his home. But bringing Joey anywhere else hadn't been an option. Even before he knew about the car, he'd known it was a very real possibility that someone had seen her last night in the lab. He wasn't going to risk dropping her off at her run-down apartment complex without protection.

Despite his exhaustion, he had tossed and turned all night. He couldn't get the vision of Laura laying on the office floor out of his head.

"So you slept well?" he asked Joey as they went up the steps.

"Oh yeah. How about you?" she asked.

"Not so great. My brain wouldn't turn off," he added. He glanced back at her once he reached the hallway. There was sympathy on her face. "I think I finally dozed off about four o'clock this morning."

Her eyes were soft and kind. "That's rough. You must be exhausted. And then Flint and I are all invading your space and whatnot."

He shrugged. "I'm okay for now. But I'll probably feel it later." He changed the subject. "My office is right down here."

"Let me grab my bag real quick. I've got a few files I might need."

Cole paused outside her room, his eyes falling on the unmade bed before she shut the door—evidence that Joey had slept just down the hall from him. If the memory of Laura's body and the events of the evening hadn't kept him awake, surely, the knowledge that Joey was just down the hall would have.

She came back out, no longer donning the fluffy robe but wearing jeans and one of his T-shirts. He vaguely remembered leaving a stack in the dresser a few months ago. It looked good on her. He cleared his throat and tore his gaze away from the way his T-shirt clung to her small frame.

"Thanks. Sorry to keep you waiting," she said.

He shook his head. "Do you need more time? A shower?"

She shook her head. "I'm good for now. After I do some work, I'll feel better about taking a break."

Cole understood that. He and Joey seemed to have that in common. Most people didn't understand his need to work so hard. She'd never made him feel bad about it though.

He stepped into the office, trying to see it through Joey's eyes. He didn't spend much time in this room, preferring to keep Zia work relegated to his office there. The walls were surrounded by tall, dark wooden bookshelves. He'd always collected books. They were one thing he wasn't afraid to spend money on. The art on his walls was chosen by a decorator. The only car he owned was nice, but not outrageous. His books though? The collection contained everything from the ripped copies of his childhood favorites to signed first editions of the classics.

He just wished he had more time to read. But all of his time had to go to Zia and the mission there. The few times he'd thought perhaps there was room in his life for something beyond work, the woman he'd dated had quickly become an irritating distraction from far more important matters.

None of them seemed to understand how important his work was. It was more than a job. It was his purpose in life. He had peace about that. But women never seemed to think that was enough. Unfortunately, most of the ones he met were only attracted to his wallet or his image. They all said they were so proud of the work he did… until it meant canceling a date or missing a call.

"Wow, this is a great room." Joey's voice snapped him out of his thoughts.

He smiled at her. "Thanks. I enjoy it." He gestured to the desk. "Here you go. Make yourself at home. It's top-of-the-line, though I'm sure it doesn't have all the bells and whistles you're used to."

Joey shrugged as she dropped her bag next to the desk. "I'm not too picky. If someone like me needs all the bells and whistles, then they've been spoiled." Her tone was one of annoyance. What did she have against people with money?

"Most of us learned on second-hand PCs and scrimped for the money to customize our own as we went. Not too many rich kids are trying to backdoor their way into the school lunch program to add money to their friends' accounts."

Cole softened, his irritation at her prejudice vanishing into sympathy. "Did you…?" He asked the question without finishing it.

Joey jerked a shoulder. "So what if I did? It was a dollar to feed your kids lunch and their deadbeat parents couldn't bother to do it. I saw one of the lunch ladies get in trouble for feeding a kid who couldn't pay." It was easy to see she was still fired up about the injustice, her chin set and her expression intense. "So I hid in the school all night and adjusted the balances."

She smiled softly, her gaze unfocused as she recounted the memory. Her fingers rested on the back of his office chair as she stood behind it. "I remember lunch tasting extra good the next day when I told my friends to go through the line." She chuckled and shook her head. "Eventually, they found out that someone was doing it, but not who. And not before I figured out other ways to help my friends. It was probably wrong. Technically stealing, I guess, but I didn't care. It was the first time I realized that the things I'd learned could be used to change something I didn't like about the world."

She looked up at him. "And there was a lot I didn't like about it. Still is," she added.

He nodded. "Yeah. I get that. There's a lot I'd like to change too." His soft words hung between them, an invisible tether that connected them. So different, yet perhaps not as incompatible as it would seem. Then he laughed. "I mean, I never hacked a computer system to do it, but to each his own."

The tension in the room broke, and Joey's laughter rang through the quiet space. There was an immense satisfaction in being the one to make her laugh. She'd just revealed a different side of herself. A softer, altruistic side. Admiring her skill, intelligence, and moxie was one thing. Connecting with her heart was another altogether. The more he knew about Josephina Rodriguez, the more he was desperate to know. How had she gone from adding money to school lunch accounts to being arrested by the FBI? How had Flint managed to get her into Raven Tech and then to follow him to Black Tower?

Joey pulled the chair out and sat down. That was his cue. "I suppose I'll leave you to it."

She nodded and turned her gaze to the screen. "Thanks. I'll be down in a bit."

Reluctant to leave, he walked toward the door. He glanced back and found Joey leaning forward, her features highlighted by the light from the screen. It was a bit unsettling to see her so at home in his private space, though it was a feeling that was not as unwelcome as he would have imagined.

She didn't look up at him. Perhaps he was losing it, simply experiencing a trauma response to the events of last night. Was he looking for connection wherever he could because he'd witnessed first-hand just how quickly life could be extinguished?

He shook his head and stepped out the door. Flint was waiting downstairs. As always, there was work to be done.

———

Joey stared at the screen, not really seeing anything. She could feel Cole's eyes on her. She couldn't look at him. As soon as he was gone, her eyes flicked to the empty doorway, wishing she hadn't missed the chance to meet his eyes again.

Two weeks ago, the prospect of sitting at Cole Kensington's personal computer would have filled her with glee. This was an opportunity she would have had to break into his house to get. She'd considered it, in fact. And here she was, at the personal invitation of the man, and trusted enough to be left entirely alone.

Her eyes flicked to the email icon and then to the storage drive on the desktop.

She blew out a breath and pulled one of her USBs out of her bag. Ignoring the email, she set aside the way the conversation with Cole had made her feel. Why had she told him about her school lunch Robin

Hood days? No one knew that. Not even Flint. And she'd told Cole what her first illegal hacking had been?

She needed to get a hold of herself. She opened the backdoor into the Zia system she'd put in place Friday before the murder, then scoured the access logs for anything significant.

She zeroed in on a suspicious entry. That name... Hadn't they already logged out? She scrolled back up. Yep, there it was. James Harlowe had scanned out at 5:21 pm. Then back out again at 5:45. Why would he come back? And how had he scanned out twice?

Unless... someone had used James's keycard to cover their own tracks. She pulled all of his records to be sure, but there was nothing out of the ordinary in his history. He didn't even work on Laura's floor, actually. She thought back to the stairwell. With the right accomplice, someone could easily access another lab.

She wrote James's name down to dig into further, and then turned back to the program. If she looked closely, she could see the footprint of her own illicit access. She skimmed the log and found a similar pattern. That hadn't been her. 6:42 pm.

It was impossible to tell who the phantom record belonged to. To anyone else, it would look like just another artifact of the system, one of a hundred events in the security log that didn't track to a specific badge.

But she knew.

How had they gotten past the Raven Tech security system?

In the six years she'd worked at Raven Tech, or in the ten years since, she'd never seen anyone able to disappear within the RT800x system the way she did.

She needed to create a list of potential contractors who would be able to accomplish something like that. For now, she closed the program and began to clean up her things. Her gaze fell on the desktop files again.

She glanced at the door. She was tucked away in the office upstairs, Cole and Flint two floors below in the kitchen.

When would she have this opportunity again? She wouldn't.

Joey pressed her lips together and clicked into the email application, rolling her eyes when the password was pre-saved in the login screen.

She skimmed as quickly as she could, glancing at the door every few moments as her nerves ratcheted higher. Cole's inbox was as orderly as the rest of him. A quick flip through the trash revealed that he opened and promptly deleted every marketing email from the gym around the corner. And the emails from the bookstore across town. Her own personal inbox was a graveyard of fifteen thousand unopened emails from stores, charities, and social media.

Only a handful of messages remained in Cole's main inbox, all unopened. But nothing looked especially interesting, although her heart squeezed seeing the same daily devotional email she received.

A notification popped up in the corner. A new message.

Senator Morris? Immediately, Joey's mind went back three months to the discovery she and Ryder had made about Senator Morris. She'd played a major role in the Syndicate targeting Fiona Raven. From what Joey could find, it all came down to money, and for Senator Morris, power.

Joey clicked into the email, eagerly taking in every word. The woman's jovial tone coupled with obvious offers of a quid pro quo made her clench her jaw.

Senator Morris was offering to throw her weight around at the FDA for Cole. She didn't mention what she wanted in return, but the insinuation was there. Cole was trading favors with the devil.

And that was enough to wipe away all the warm feelings Joey was harboring about her current employer. Someone was targeting Zia Pharmaceuticals and his Alzheimer's therapy project. But getting into bed with Katrina Morris? Hard to feel very sympathetic.

With disgust, she marked the email unread and closed out of the program. Then she installed a very discrete remote monitoring program. As it was finishing, she heard footsteps on the stairs. She tapped her fingers nervously, watching the upload bar inch across the screen. "Come on, baby. Go, go, go."

She pulled the USB from the computer just as Cole stepped through the door.

"Hey, how's it going?"

"Good. I didn't find much. Is Flint still here? I need to run something past him."

Cole shook his head. "He ran out. Jessica called. Something about the baby shower?"

"Oh." Joey fumbled with her bag. All of a sudden, she was very aware that she was alone with Cole Kensington, and she was also doubly sure that he was not the guy he seemed to be.

"You can probably call him." Cole walked toward the desk. "Do you mind? I'm going to take care of a few things while we've got a minute."

"Sure. I'll go downstairs."

"You're welcome to stay up here. Then I can hear what you say to Flint."

Joey froze. "Umm, oh. Okay, yeah."

Why did he want to hear? Did he suspect something?

She moved away from him, circling the desk the opposite way he was coming from. She sat in one of the large, cushioned leather chairs across the room and pulled out her phone.

She heard a scoff from Cole.

"What's wrong?"

He shook his head. "Just checking my email. Don't worry about it too much."

"Come on, let's go downstairs and make a plan."

# CHAPTER FIFTEEN

JARED WALKED through the door around one o'clock, carrying takeout bags from The Screaming Peach. "I come bearing gifts."

Joey smiled at his offering. "You're the best."

"Just doing my job, ma'am."

Joey stood up from the couch and met him at the kitchen counter to unload the food. "Cole's upstairs taking a shower," she told Jared.

"I'll just throw his in the fridge."

Joey unwrapped a sandwich and sipped the peach lemonade for a moment. She'd been down here for ten minutes alone, contemplating her next decision about Cole. No matter how attracted to him she was, or how good he might seem at times, she couldn't forget the fact that he had this other side.

A darker side.

"Can I ask you a question, Jared?"

"I guess so," he responded.

"Why do you work for Cole? What's the story between you two?"

Jared glanced at the stairs, as though waiting for Cole to make an entrance, but they remained empty. He looked back at her.

"I don't know that it's my place to tell you Cole's story."

Joey pursed her lips thoughtfully. "Well, then just tell me your story," she suggested.

Jared took a seat at the other end of the bar.

"You gotta understand, I didn't have a family like Cole did. When he showed up in the group home, it was a temporary thing, you know? I'd been there for two years, since my last foster placement kicked me out."

Joey struggled to keep up. She didn't want to interrupt or ask too many questions, but they were swirling as he spoke. Cole had been in a group home? That had never come up anywhere that she'd been able to find.

"Cole was the new kid. And a rich one. I mean, none of us had a family. But at least he had money, you know? The other kids didn't like that so much."

Joey's heart sank for Cole in that situation. She was enraptured by the story and silently encouraged Jared to continue with a nod.

"We sort of hit it off. He wasn't there for long, but we were tight. I watched his back, I guess."

"I'm glad he had you," she offered.

The corner of Jared's mouth quirked up. "Yeah, well. That was when it all went down and I got arrested. It was Cole's turn to have my back, I guess."

"Will you tell me about it?"

He sighed and leaned back. "Ah, why not? There was this big shot lawyer that used to come around the home. Acted like he wanted to give back. Told the staff he wanted to mentor the kids and all that crap." Jared ran his hand over his short hair. "Basically, the guy was a scumbag. I found him with some of the younger boys. Making them… do stuff they didn't want to do."

Joey's gut rolled and she tossed her sandwich to the counter. "Oh, sweetie."

Jared shrugged. "It is what it is. I was seventeen at the time. I talked to Cole and we were both so angry. I knew the odds. I was going to end up in jail anyway. I decided it was probably as good a cause as any."

Her heart broke for the young, hopeless man he must have been to make that decision.

"There wasn't any denying to the police that I beat the snot out of him. He was in the hospital for months, and he still lives in a nursing home." He looked toward the stairs again. "Cole used his trust fund or whatever to pay for my lawyer so I didn't have the public defender. Got me a good deal, all things considered."

Joey shook her head. "I'm so sorry, Jared." She had definitely misjudged him. With limited information, she'd assumed Jared's felony conviction meant he was a bad guy. So what else was she missing?

"It's okay. I'm okay now. It's pretty hard to get a decent job with a record like mine, but working for Cole isn't a bad gig."

She smiled. "He can be a little bossy, I'd say."

Jared laughed. "Yeah, he can. But he's got a good heart."

The words, spoken by a convicted felon with clear admiration and trust, settled over her. Did she believe him?

"How can you be sure, Jared?"

He leaned in. "I see a lot of Cole that other people don't see. He might be uptight and work too much. Sometimes, he's too demanding or insensitive. But he would never do anything that wasn't above board. He wouldn't compromise his integrity for anything."

"Not even for the cure?" That was the rub. If Cole had convictions but was willing to set them aside, get in bed with Senator Morris and bribe a judge for the Syndicate, then those convictions were meaningless.

Jared shook his head. "Not even for that. I'm telling you, he's a better man than me. Even though that dude was a total dirtbag, Cole pays for his nursing home through some anonymous thing. Says it's our responsibility, since I made the choice to handle it like I did. I don't know about that. I like to think I'd handle it differently today, but I'm not sure. The guy was married to a judge. A lawyer himself. Upstanding member of society and all that. If we'd gone to the police, I'd bet Cole's entire fortune on nothing changing."

"What are you betting my fortune on this time?"

Joey jumped at Cole's sudden intrusion to their conversation.

"Oh, you know. The Red Sox making the World Series this year," Jared said with a wink.

"Yeah, right."

They finished their lunch, and Joey walked back through everything Jared had shared with her. The payoffs to the judge in Salem… She'd double check, but it was all starting to add up to a very different picture than the one she'd painted initially.

Cole smiled at her between bites of his sandwich. "You okay?"

She nodded. "Yeah. Just thinking."

"I was thinking we could work on that report this afternoon?" Cole was relaxed and cheerful. He didn't seem to be hiding anything. Now that she was looking with fresh information, perhaps he never had been.

They went up to the office, and Cole pulled a chair around so they could both see the computer screen.

Her eyes flicked to the email application. Was the email from Senator Morris still in his inbox? Or had it quickly and efficiently been dealt with and filed?

Even as the cynical thought crossed her mind, she dismissed it. It was time to face the facts.

She tipped her head back and closed her eyes.

"What's wrong?" came Cole's voice from right next to her.

Joey shook her head. "I'm an idiot." She looked up and met Cole's look of amusement.

He smiled. "I'm sure that's not true."

"I think I owe you an apology."

He frowned. "Why?"

She sat up and leaned forward on her knees. "What have you heard about the Syndicate?"

Cole raised his eyebrows. "Not much. Flint has

mentioned the name once or twice. I've heard whispers other places."

"I thought you were part of it," Joey admitted with a wince.

Cole laughed. "Why on earth would you think that?"

Joey stood up, unable to stay still. She paced behind the armchair. "I don't know, Cole. What am I supposed to think? Everything I can find on the Syndicate confirms that they are some of the richest, most powerful people in the country. And here you are…"

"So anyone who is rich is suddenly evil, Joey?"

She gave him a pointed look. "You tell me. You run in those circles more than I do."

He shook his head. "That's ridiculous and completely unfair. Whatever the Syndicate is part of, I have nothing to do with it."

"I realize that now. But you have to see from my perspective." She counted things off on her fingers. All the connections that tied him to people inside the Syndicate. "You're on the board of Hamilton House with Tripp Harrington—confirmed Syndicate member. Senator Collins donated a million dollars to your foundation—confirmed Syndicate. Your personal bodyguard has a felony record."

He shot upright, "Hey, I told you—"

She kept going. "You share a private jet with Ferrell Thornsby from Thornsby Oil! You own a house in Key West, right next to Patrick Derulo from QuinTech Missiles. You're sending payments to a federal judge in Salem."

His eyes widened but she kept going. "You sponsor a scholarship that went to the granddaughter of Matthew Stoops."

"Am I supposed to know who that is?" His voice was laced with outrage and confusion.

"He's the flipping Director of the CIA, Cole!" She threw her hands in the air. "I could go on. Every time I dig into the lives of Syndicate members, you show up. And earlier today… What am I supposed to think when you're getting friendly emails from Senator Morris? The same woman who arranged the entire attack on Flint's sister, Fiona?" She immediately wished she could pull the words back and swallow them. Even she admitted reading his personal emails was crossing a line.

Cole's eyes widened? "That was Senator Morris?"

Joey nodded. Maybe he wouldn't connect the dots and realize she—

"Wait a second. How did you know about that email?"

Joey pressed her lips together. "Umm…"

"Joey," he growled.

She held up her hands in surrender. "I might have snuck a peek at your inbox. But it wasn't even really hacking. You had the password saved! Anyone could have done it. It wasn't like reading your emails at work. That was way harder."

———

Cole raised his eyebrows, and Joey clapped a hand over her mouth.

His head was pounding and his fists clenched tightly. Anger and disbelief left no room in his thoughts for anything else.

"You're kidding. Tell me you're kidding. You didn't spend your time inside Zia, the company I invited you inside to help me— Tell me you didn't spend that time investigating me instead of finding the mole and the person who murdered Laura!" His volume escalated until he was outright yelling at her.

Joey paused next to the armchair. "To be fair, I was doing both."

Her quiet rebuttal had the tension and fury melting away. Leave it to Joey to respond with a snarky comment in the face of his ire. Cole's fingers came to his hair, tangled in it, and pulled it straight up. "What am I going to do with you, Joey?"

She winced and lifted her shoulders. "Forgive me?"

Cole shook his head. "Why should I? You've been lying to me this entire time! I trusted you. I let you into my company. I brought you into my home! Dang it, Joey. I thought—"

He paused. He'd been about to say he thought they shared something. That he cared about her. He'd actually let her in, not just to his company, but to his life. And then to find out that the entire thing was just a lie to her?

Joey sighed. "Since meeting you, my gut has been telling me that I was wrong. That you were different…"

"Was Flint in on it? Did he send you on this mission?" The possibility that one of his closest friends suspected him of this evil and corruption nearly brought him to his knees.

Joey's expression of surprise seemed completely genuine though. She shook her head adamantly.

"No. Raven had nothing to do with this. He's never doubted you for a minute. I'm so sorry, Cole. I just needed to be sure."

Cole heard the desperation in her words, thought

about all he knew about her and her past. The string of coincidences she listed off was significant. But there was nothing more there—just coincidences.

"If there is anything I've learned since we met, it's that you are strong-willed and determined." He was standing close to her now. "Honestly, if I'd seen the same things as you, I probably would have assumed the worst too. And for the record, Senator Morris is under the mistaken impression that I would let someone strongarm the FDA to approve something that wasn't ready. Even if she could somehow force them to ignore science and push through the approval, which she couldn't—"

"That's debatable," Joey interjected.

"Well, *even if* she could, I wouldn't want her to."

"Jared did say you were a man of integrity."

Cole grinned. "He said that, huh?"

She nodded. "I'm pretty used to not trusting people…"

"You can trust me, Joey." His voice was a whisper, almost a plea. He desperately wanted her trust. To be searched and be found worthy of being within this remarkable woman's inner circle. His eyes dropped to the gentle curve of her cheek, his fingers itching to trace the smooth skin there.

She nodded. "I know I can. I do. Even if you are rich." Her eyes sparked with laughter.

At her admission, and to silence her quip, Cole was helpless to do anything other than capture her lips with his own. Somehow, between taunting him with little pranks and sneaking into his personal affairs, Josephina had inched her way in between the strongholds of his defenses. They crumbled now, nothing but ruins of the walls he'd built, brought to the ground by the earth-shaking power of Joey in his arms.

He tasted her, savoring the way she tipped her head up to meet him. His hand cupped her cheek, tracing a line with his thumb. Despite his best intentions, he'd trusted Joey enough to see the real him. And she hadn't run scared. Of the dreams that some women mocked or the single-willed focus with which he approached his goals. She understood him better than anyone ever had. And after a thorough investigation—the kind only Joey could orchestrate—she trusted him.

Slowly, he broke the kiss but held her close. Her eyes were unfocused, shuttered slightly. Her lips still parted from the kiss. His smile lifted on one side, thinking of her smart mouth and how satisfying it was to silence it with that kiss.

Joey looked up at him. "That was… um. That was…"

"Perfect?" he supplied.

Joey chuckled. "Yeah. Kind of." She touched her fingers to her lips, and he felt the pride expand in his chest. That was the kind of kiss he never wanted to forget. The kind of core memory he was trying so hard to preserve for himself and others in his fight against Alzheimer's.

He groped for words, unsure how to move forward after that kiss had totally shaken his world. "Joey, I, uh…"

Joey seemed to startle and she stepped back. Immediately, he missed the closeness of her body. "Oh, right. We should get to work, right?"

He nodded and exhaled. "Yeah, probably."

# CHAPTER
# SIXTEEN

WHEN JOEY WALKED into work on Monday morning, Will was already at the security desk. He gave her an imperceptible head nod as she met his eyes. Then he was looking elsewhere, nodding to something the other guard said.

When she got off on the fourth floor, she tried to hide her surprise at Tank's presence in the cubicle next to hers. Unlike her own first day, he already had a computer and an ID badge.

"Good morning. I'm Travis," he said. "From the internal audit team. Don't mind me at all. I'm just observing." She could tell Tank was trying to put on a friendly demeanor, but he was still gruff and intimidating.

Joey tried to stifle a laugh. "Nice to meet you, Travis. I'm Joey."

She knew that Tank couldn't tell anyone what an auditor did, but she felt so much better knowing that he was sitting next to her.

With Ryder downstairs monitoring the cameras and Tank sitting nearby, she felt as safe as she had during the weekend—first at Cole's house and then behind the technologically fortified walls of Black Tower.

The memory of staying with Cole made her heart flutter. Cole had been a perfect gentleman as they worked on the false documents from her office. Somewhat to Joey's dismay, actually. She'd been hoping for a repeat performance of the kiss that had rocked her to her core. But Cole had apparently shifted back into business-mode. It was fine. She knew it was better that way. But she couldn't help but get distracted by the way the stubble on his chin had grown by Sunday afternoon, replacing his clean-cut workaholic billionaire vibe with a slightly disheveled version she wanted to lay on the beach with.

Which a foolish fantasy, she knew. Cole Kensington didn't lay on the beach. He didn't even take vacations, despite the house in Florida waiting for him whenever he could want it.

She settled in at her desk and tucked the flash drive with the false documents into her sleeve. "I'm going to do a quick monitoring review on the server room," she announced to Ben, with a glance to Tank.

He stood. "Uh, Joey. I think that's something I'd like to observe. For the audit." He cleared his throat.

"Is that really necessary?" Ben looked up from his computer after he spoke, and his eyes widened as he took in Tank's size.

Tank crossed his arms. "I'm the auditor, right?"

Ben nodded, shrinking back into his chair. "Uh, yes, sir. Enjoy your audit."

"Let's go then. Server room is this way."

She held back her laughter until the server room door was closed behind them. She used Tank as a support as she doubled over in laughter. "Oh man. His face. It never gets old."

Tank chuckled, though there was no smile behind it. "He seems like a real winner," he said.

Joey finished laughing. "Yeah. He's too caught up in his own stuff to worry about anyone else. He's already forgotten we're in here."

She grabbed the flash drive and quickly uploaded the false reports. They'd be distributed through the same automated systems as any normal results. Except this set was specially created to make it look like the drug had even better results than predicted. Joey was hoping that whoever was altering tests wouldn't be able to resist trying to mess with these ones.

"How's your house coming along?" she asked Tank to fill the silence.

He shrugged. "Not bad. Still more painting to do. But it's coming along."

Joey smirked. He'd shown her pictures of the paint colors in the house he purchased. Apparently, the previous owners had teenage daughters and let them choose their own colors. It resulted in a lime-green bedroom with zebra print painted on one wall and another room that was hot pink and orange. The rest of the house wasn't much better, with dark-maroon walls and floral wallpaper in every bathroom.

She shook her head. "I know you got a good deal on the place, but I don't know how you haven't just hired someone by now." It had been six months.

"I don't want anyone in my house," he growled. "It's bad enough that I let you talk me into a housekeeper."

Joey laughed. "I've seen your locker at work. Trust me, she's worth the money. How's the new girl working out? What was her name again?"

Tank shrugged. "Katie? Something like that."

Joey remembered the background check she ran. "That's right. Kaylie. Kaylie Richards."

"Sure. That sounds right. I pretty much never see her. But I come home on Tuesdays and the house is clean, so that works for me."

Joey rolled her eyes. "That sounds nice. I wish I could afford someone. My apartment is a wreck." Not to mention that every spare dollar from her paycheck was already accounted for. She was still literally paying the price for some poor choices and innocent people she'd hurt before Flint found her.

Tank grunted. "I'm sure it's fine. After this job, you'll probably be able to buy a new place. I heard the bonus is the biggest we've ever accepted."

Joey raised her eyebrows. "Flint hasn't mentioned it."

"Probably because he knows you won't want it anyway."

"What does that mean?" She gave him a confused look. Why wouldn't she want the money?

Tank shrugged. "Everybody knows you're not a fan of rich people."

Joey frowned at him. "Really?"

"Well, you don't exactly make it a secret."

Joey waited for Tank to expand, but true to form, he stayed quiet.

"How much is this bonus, exactly?" It must be big to have everyone at BTS talking about it.

"I heard a million. But that could have just been Jackson shooting his mouth off."

She rolled her eyes. Of course it would be Jackson. Odds were fifty-fifty whether what he said was true or not. "I'll ask Flint."

"Does it matter?"

Tank's question made her pause. Did it? She was already doing everything in her power to help Cole protect this project. Because despite his money and the way he'd achieved his success, she believed him about the potential for this therapy. She even believed what he said about why he did things the way he did.

As much as she hated to admit it, her first impressions of Cole had been all wrong.

"No. It doesn't."

She wasn't doing this for money. She wasn't even doing it because Flint asked her to. After everything that had happened, she was still working on this because she cared about Cole. She cared about the research having the chance to move forward and change the world and for Cole to have a battle victory in his fight.

Million dollars or not, she was in this to the end.

———

"Mr. Kensington, you need to see this!" Cole frowned at the interruption. It was unlike Janet to interrupt him by coming directly into the office. Her voice held a combination of emotions he couldn't decipher.

"What's going on? I've got to get through this proposal." He was curious and trying not to be unkind, but he really did have pressing matters to take care of.

"President Walters has been shot." Her voice echoed disbelief and horror.

Cole leaned back into his chair as though he'd been shoved. A thousand questions ran through his mind, but he couldn't seem to make any reach his mouth. Janet disappeared out the door, and then a message popped up on his computer from their instant message chain. A link.

He clicked it and was immediately taken to the live video stream for WBC News. The anchor's voice came through his speakers.

"For those who are just joining us, we have a rapidly developing situation here. We have confirmation that President Walters has been shot. This took place about forty-five minutes ago. The President was in Florida to visit the site of the damage and flooding from Hurricane Patricia last month. All we know right now is that we have received confirmation that she was struck and is receiving medical treatment at Orlando Regional Hospital. The shooter has not been apprehended at this time."

Cole listened to them repeat this same information, with very little variation in the script, a few more times before he let it fade into the background. So many questions. President Walters had been elected to her second term last fall, making her not only the first woman president, but the first to be elected twice.

"...received word that Vice-President Coulter has been sworn in, per the 25th amendment, and is currently the acting President of the United States. He is expected to make a statement to the country later this evening."

Cole let the droning of the anchors fade again. He'd met President Walters a few times when she was a senator and since she was elected. From his own impressions and everything he knew, she was a godly woman who refused to allow politics to get in the way of her integrity. It would be a devastating loss to the country if she died.

He prayed for her recovery quickly, then said

another for Harrison Coulter. He knew the man in passing. Coulter's wife was actually the sister of Ross McClain's wife, who was the cofounder of Black Tower Security.

Janet ran back inside. "Did you see?"

He nodded wordlessly.

"I can't believe it," she said. "She was such an incredible woman."

"She's not dead, yet, right?" he clarified.

Janet flushed. "Oh my, you're right. I shouldn't talk like that. But I heard that it doesn't look very promising."

Cole shook his head. "Speculation and rumors are never reliable. Let's just pray and wait. And work, I suppose."

"How can you work at a time like this?" Janet said, appalled.

Cole tensed. "It's not like the FBI needs my help, nor the doctors. I'm going to focus on what is under my control, and that is this company and my work. I suggest you do the same. Draft a note to our staff recommending they take a moment to pray but that our work is as important as ever."

He frowned as Janet shook her head. "I don't know, Mr. Kensington. I don't think there will be much work happening."

She was probably right. He exhaled and ran a hand through his hair. A glance at the clock told him it was nearly 3 pm. "Fine. Send a note and send everyone home, but tomorrow we come back ready to work."

Janet nodded. "Yes, sir."

# CHAPTER SEVENTEEN

COLE PRESSED his fingers to his eyes as the beginning notes of a migraine began to form there. Stress. He shut the newscast off and glanced at the proposal still open on his computer. Even if everyone else in his office was leaving, he would be staying.

A knock on his door interrupted him about an hour later. He glanced up. "Joey. What are you doing here?"

He looked around at his office for any witnesses, despite knowing it was empty. "You can't be here, Joey. Someone might see you."

Joey just stared at him. "You know the entire building is empty, right?"

"Not entirely," he said with a pointed gaze.

She stepped through the door. "Yeah, well. I figured you'd still be here, so I came up."

"I'm really glad you did." He wasn't sure he was ready to analyze the depth of that statement, but seeing Joey at his door had lifted the weight of the rest of the day.

She sat across from him and crossed her legs. A red stiletto heel caught his eye. "How do you walk in those?"

She laughed. "Practice. And strong calves." She waited. "And I keep a pair of sneakers in my purse. But I figured if I was coming to the boss's office, I should look the part."

"Even if no one sees?"

She nodded. "You saw," she said with a smirk.

Heat rolled up his neck, and Cole tugged on his already unbuttoned collar. "Everything in place for the false report?"

"Uploaded this morning. Now we just need you to hint at it in your meeting with the directors. We'll see who bites and falls into the trap door I left behind."

He shook his head. "I don't know anything about all that, but I sure hope it works. I've got the FDA breathing down my neck, and I don't know what I'll do if I can't prove the project still has merit."

Joey frowned. "Can they just shut it down, or what?"

"Kind of? The whole process is super long, but yeah, they could hold up any further trials if they think the results don't seem to warrant further study. And if our results are radically different from the same research at other places, even if I'm pretty sure those results are bogus, then it calls all of our trials into question. And," he continued as the realization struck, "it won't just put a damper on this project. It'll make all of our trials circumspect. We'll be under a microscope for everything."

"Aren't you already?" Joey leaned forward. "Like, they're already looking at everything super closely, right? They're not just approving things willy-nilly."

"That's true. But it's different when they trust you. We've got a reputation for upholding the highest research standards and objective trials. I don't want to jeopardize that."

He stood up and paced behind his desk. "I know why they have to play gatekeeper. But sometimes… The entire process is so frustrating. It takes months to analyze data. Months to hold a meeting to vote. And meanwhile, everything we're doing is essentially paused."

"Yeah, but they're keeping people safe. Protecting

them from companies who might be tempted to rush a drug to production to start earning back their research costs."

He turned quickly. "Is that what you think about me? My work?" The idea that Joey still harbored such negative feelings about his work integrity was like a punch to the gut.

Joey shook her head. "No, Cole. Not you… I mean, maybe I did to begin with. But I see that I had misjudged you. Maybe it's not every company, but you can't argue that there are others who care more about profit than they do about science or helping people." She wasn't backing down. "They jack up the cost of basic prescription medications until they bankrupt people simply for being born with a certain condition."

He knew exactly what she was talking about. It was a disgusting process, one that President Walters had vowed to put an end to. "Why do you think I bought Placana? That jerk Lionel was charging insurance companies four grand a month for a drug that cost $4 to produce. And he was putting every bit of it into his own pocket."

He hadn't publicized it, and the sale would be announced in a week or two. It was a stupid business decision, but one that had given him immense satis-faction.

Joey paused. "I heard it was a possibility, but it's true?"

He nodded. "Every person who is on Lovenidia will have their prescription costs cut by 90% next month. That particular drug will still be very prof-itable for ZiaTech, but it will not bankrupt another family just trying to take care of their kids. It's one thing to cover the expenses of research and develop-ment. It's another to intentionally price gouge people."

Emotion flickered across Joey's face, each one undecipherable. She sniffed, and he stepped closer, coming around his desk toward her. "Are you okay?"

She shook her head and brought her hands to her eyes, wiping away tears. "I'm okay. I just... I'm really glad you're doing that." Her words were tight, and he could see she was fighting back more tears.

He sat in the chair next to hers, his hand coming to rest on her knee. "Of course... I'm just glad I can do things like this. Most people are powerless against people and companies like that."

"Yeah, it sucks." Joey's words were laced with laughter. It was nice to see her smiling through the tears, though it was mostly hidden from his view as she kept her eyes on the floor in front of them. She sniffed again and turned to him. Her eyes shimmered as they searched his. "Thank you," she whispered.

Cole didn't know what to say. One thing was certain. He'd buy a hundred scummy companies if it meant Joey would continue to look at him with the joy and approval and respect for him radiating on her face right now.

"What is it? Please tell me," he pleaded, desperate to understand why this meant so much.

Joey swiped at a tear and shook her head. She took a deep breath and let it out with a shaky exhale. "It's fine. I'm okay. Just caught me by surprise. It's a good thing you're doing." She looked around the office. "Here, this. All of it." She laid her hand on his where it still rested on her knee.

Cole had received accolades and admiration before. People who placed him and his mission on a pedestal, sometimes because they genuinely supported it and others because they thought boosting his ego would help them get what they wanted from him. Usually money.

He nodded. He turned her hand over in his, studying the interplay of their fingers. He moved his gaze to her face. Joey's approval wasn't empty or self-serving. She'd shown that she wouldn't placate him with praise. She didn't even want to accept the few perks of his lifestyle he had tried to offer.

He wiped the trace of a tear from her cheek with his hand, sliding his thumb across the soft curve of her cheek. His hand trailed down, slipping behind her neck and resting under her ear. She tipped her head, gently allowing him access.

He'd relived the kiss in his townhouse a hundred times since Saturday. Gone back and forth, telling himself that it was a fluke. Then deciding that he should march down to the fourth floor and declare his feelings before convincing himself that even if it was real, it would never work. She wouldn't want him, and he couldn't jeopardize this operation for something that wouldn't last.

All those arguments warred within him, fighting for the top billing in his mind as he leaned in to kiss her.

The moment his lips touched hers though, the arguments all disappeared, fading into the fog as the overwhelming sensation of kissing her took center stage.

———

Joey sighed, melting into the kiss. She leaned into Cole's touch, letting everything inside that had been just slightly ajar click into place, like the tumblers of a padlock. He was the thief, slowly wiggling his way beyond her defenses, one by one. And on the other side of that connection she'd found she trusted him. The way she trusted Flint. The way she'd trusted others and ended up hurt.

Hearing that he was dismantling Placana and correcting the predatory medication pricing had disarmed her entirely. Lovenidia was the drug her sister had taken until they couldn't afford it anymore. She'd died at just ten years old without Lovenidia to help her body guard against the impact of her disease.

It was a wrong she'd never been able to right. But Cole had, even without knowing the impact it would have on her. Cole had power now that she'd handed over. Willingly or not, she had given him power to hurt her. But she trusted that he wouldn't.

Every doubt, every assumption she had, he'd quietly proven to be false.

She leaned into the kiss, unlike any other she'd experienced without any pretense left between them. Cole looked at her like she was the most incredible thing he'd ever seen. When he looked at her, she was beautiful and powerful and this man who somehow remained truly good, despite his wealth, power, and good looks... He wanted her. Broken and cynical and sometimes pushy. He wanted her.

Joey kissed him back, teasing his lips with her own and savoring the feel of his soft lips on hers and his raspy stubble brushing her cheek. Her fingers found his hair, and she buried them there.

The jarring ring of his phone interrupted them, and they sprang apart, like teenagers caught making out at the front door after curfew.

He frowned at the phone before answering with it on speaker. "Flint?"

"Is Joey with you?" He spoke quickly, and there was something in his tone. Worry?

"I'm here," she said quickly, trying to reassure him. "What's up?"

"I need you at BTS. Now." Oh. That wasn't worry she heard. That was Flint's command center voice, the one he put on when the situation was about to go crazy and someone needed to keep things together.

"I'll be there. Thirty minutes," she promised.

Cole hung up the call.

She stood quickly, straightening her skirt. "I better go," she said.

He rolled his eyes. "Let's go. I'll text Jared on the way down."

"You don't have to drive me," she insisted.

"Of course I do. Don't forget, we're still at high alert, Joey. Just because we got to come to work today doesn't mean things are normal." He punched the button to call the elevator. "We've still got a dead body and a sabotaged drug trial."

How could she forget?

Oh yeah, probably the kiss.

When they reached the first floor, Joey saw Tank sitting in the lobby. He slowly rose from a tiny modern chair that looked like it was about to surrender under the assault of his body mass.

"Where have you been, Joey?" Tank's question was barked as much as it was asked, which wasn't unusual. But there was extra agitation there this time. "Raven and Ross have been trying to get a hold of you for an hour."

She looked around helplessly. "No phones upstairs. You know that. Why are you here anyway?"

"You're not supposed to be alone, remember?" Tank's gaze slid to Kensington. "Although, apparently, you've got that taken care of. You'll have to take your date another night. I've got orders to bring her to Black Tower."

"I'm taking her to Black Tower now, Mr. Olson. Would you like to ride with us?"

Joey's mouth fell open, and she turned to Cole. In the five years she'd known Tank, she'd never heard him called anything but the moniker. Sometimes, she forgot he had a real name. Anthony Olson. She was honestly impressed that Cole knew it. And remembered it.

Tank grunted in response. The testosterone-fueled territorial vibes were starting to give her a headache. Tank turned to Joey, looking for her to make the call. She smiled softly and reached for Cole's hand. "It's okay. He's a good guy."

Tank looked apprehensive, then shrugged. "If you say so."

Joey squeezed Cole's hand. "You don't have to come. I'll be safe with him."

Cole smiled. "I don't doubt that. But I'd like to come. I'd like to know what is so urgent too."

After another short power struggle, Joey rode to BTS in Cole's town car, with Tank leading the way in the imposing black SUV. It was rumored to be armored as well as the presidential motorcade, but that was something Miranda handled as their logistics expert. Knowing her connections, she'd probably purchased it directly from the secret service the last time they upgraded their own fleet.

"Any idea what this is about?" Cole's question

echoed her own as they made their way around DC to Alexandria.

Joey had been flipping through her phone, catching up on the notifications from the outside world. It was so strange to be without the device while she was inside Zia.

"None." Her messages revealed Flint's attempts to get ahold of her. She even had missed calls from Ross McClain, who she rarely interacted with. Flint might be the operational leader of BTS, but Ross McClain was the one steering the ship, using his numerous government contacts to win business and his wife's women's defense outreach to find pro-bono work.

Why would Ross be calling her? Whatever this meeting was about, it had to be big.

# CHAPTER
# EIGHTEEN

COLE SAW the surprise on Flint's face when they all walked into the conference room.

"Cole, I didn't realize you came too. This is really confidential BTS business," he explained apologetically.

He understood, truly, but it didn't stop him from pushing back. He and Flint were close enough friends that he was willing to risk the confrontation.

"If this concerns Joey, then it concerns me."

Flint shook his head. "She works for me, Cole. Don't forget that."

"Excuse me. *She* is standing right here and doesn't appreciate being ignored." She looked between them with disappointment.

Joey's admonishment brought a wave of embarrassment. He was acting like a jealous, protective boyfriend. He didn't even know what to call their relationship, but Joey was right.

"I'm sorry. You're right. This should be up to you."

Flint scoffed, and Joey smiled. "I'm fine, Cole. Flint is right. This is my job. Why don't you go meet Dolores and wait for me? We can go grab dinner after I'm done here." She turned to Flint. "Assuming I won't be here all night?"

"This meeting will be about twenty minutes, but you'll have some work to do."

Cole tried to hide his disappointment. "I'll talk to you after the meeting, and we can make a plan, okay?"

Joey nodded. Her eyes spoke volumes though. Even if he came across as a fool, she wanted him here, and that was enough.

Cole backtracked his steps to the lobby. He'd barely noticed the gray-haired woman sitting at the reception desk when they came in.

"Kicked you out, did they?" Her voice was raspy and weathered, like she'd smoked a pack of cigarettes a day for thirty years.

He nodded. "I'm Cole."

"Oh, I know who you are. Dolores Pinkman, at your service."

He shook her hand. "Nice to meet you, Dolores. Have you worked at Black Tower very long?"

"Two years or so. I thought I was going to retire and live a nice quiet life, you know." She leaned in and winked. "Turns out, that's as boring as afternoon tea. Flint convinced me to come work for him."

Cole chuckled. "He can be very convincing, can't he?" It was something Cole was grateful for. When he'd been invited to join a Bible study for business owners, he figured it would be real estate agents and insurance salesmen. But he and Flint had hit it off. Not many people could relate to running large corporations. What had started as a weekly early morning coffee meeting had transformed into a friendship that lasted more than a decade now.

And had introduced him to Joey.

"What did you do before? Did you work for Flint at Raven Tech?"

Dolores laughed, a cackle that erupted inside the quiet lobby. "Not exactly. I was an intelligence analyst."

Cole raised his eyebrows. "Analyst, huh?"

She winked. "Absolutely."

While it was certainly possible that Flint had

recruited a former intelligence analyst to man the front desk at Black Tower, Cole had the sneaking suspicion that there was more to Dolores's story.

"Tell me about you, Cole Kensington. Rumor has it that you're sweet on our Josephina?" Dolores's eyes sparkled with mischief.

Cole felt the heat in his cheeks, and he couldn't fight the smile that spread across his face at the question. Somehow he knew he was about to tell this unsuspecting motherly figure far more than he would have intended.

———

Once Cole was out of the room, Joey took a seat at the table. Ross McClain sat at the head, with Flint to his right and Will Gilbert to his left. Tank took a seat next to her.

"What's going on?"

Ross nodded. "I'm sure you've seen the news. The President was shot and it isn't looking good. She is still in surgery."

The door opened to her left. Jackson Kelley tiptoed in and pulled out his seat, setting an energy drink in front of him.

"Sorry I'm late," he offered.

She rolled her eyes. Ross simply nodded and continued his briefing.

"With Madame President incapacitated, Vice President Coulter has been sworn in. He's married to my sister-in-law."

Joey nodded. She knew there was a connection there, but she hadn't been sure exactly what it was. "What do you need?"

Flint spoke up. "We have reason to believe the attempted assassination was orchestrated by the Syndicate."

"What?" Jackson and Tank both started asking questions. Joey watched the dynamics in the room. Will sat stoically next to Flint. He was unsurprised.

"Where is this information coming from?" Joey was struggling to come to terms with this. She was the one who gathered intel around here.

"I'm afraid we can't share that at this time," Will said firmly.

Joey shook her head. "This is crazy. I've been working on untangling the Syndicate for over a year. If there is information you're not sharing, then you're putting all of us in danger!"

Ross held up a hand. "Harrison Coulter is a good man and I trust him. He has requested Black Tower conduct an independent operation to capture the shooter after he is identified. Will, you'll be leading Operation Blue smoke along with Tank, Jackson, and Ryder."

Joey's mouth fell open. "We're going after the most wanted man in America? Why?"

"There is reason to believe the Syndicate orchestrated the attack with inside information. Harrison wants to keep it close to the vest, outside official channels, and free from any potential security breaches." Ross said. "Joey, we need to be inside the FBI and secret service systems so we know what they know when they know it. We do have Agent Roscoe inside, and we trust him. You'll be operational support when the time comes. I don't think I need to say that this is our highest priority."

Joey froze. "You want me to infiltrate the feds? You can't be serious. Raven, you're okay with this?"

Flint met her eyes across the table. "Joey, I know this is asking a lot…"

She scoffed. "You think? Do you not remember how we met? What I was doing?"

Her friend and mentor nodded. "I do. And I understand why you might want to say no."

"Dang right I want to say no. Fifteen years ago, my *team,* my *family* had me hack the FBI. And then they hung me out to dry." She felt the anger and hurt and disappointment wash over her as strongly as it had so many years ago. "You're the only reason I'm not locked in some federal prison with an hour of yard time and no access to tech."

His eyes were kind, imploring her to understand. "I wouldn't ask if this wasn't important."

She wanted to say yes. She always said yes to Flint. But this? It was asking too much. "I can't do it, Rave. What if I get caught?"

"You won't get caught, Joey. You're the best I've ever seen. And you're far more experienced now than you were back then. More careful."

Well, that was true. She'd thought she was careful before, but getting caught by the FBI after her hack was a lesson she didn't need to be taught twice.

Ross spoke. "I agree with Raven. But"—he pointed to the black portfolio in front of him—"I do have a signed Get Out of Jail Free card from the acting President of the United States for any crimes that may or may not be committed during this black op."

Jackson let out a low whistle.

She looked back at Flint, her certainty waffling at the new revelation.

He met her gaze, his confidence unwavering.

"We're not going to hang you out to dry, Joey. We've got you. Always."

Her mind was spinning. This was huge, of course. Going after the presidential assassin? And if there was no risk of a federal felony, it made the whole thing a little easier to swallow. "But what about Zia? What about Cole?"

Flint lifted his shoulders slightly. "We'll make it work, Joey. Don't worry."

Whatever Flint was saying, she didn't buy it. It was obvious Cole's project was going to get dropped until this one was resolved. She couldn't let that happen to him. And the trap was already laid, so there was no going back.

She was just going to have to find a way to balance it. She would just have to do both operations at once.

"That's all for now. The team is on standby. This could happen at a moment's notice."

The meeting ended, and Joey started toward the lobby to catch Cole. Their dinner date was going to have to wait.

A hand on her arm made her stop. She turned to find Will. "Got a second?"

He tugged her to an alcove in the hallway outside the conference room.

"I need you to do something, Joey." Will was always intense, but his expression was guarded and he kept his voice low.

"Yeah, of course. What do you need?"

Will took a deep breath, looking down the hall again as though making sure no one could hear them. "I need you to deep dive on Coulter. I need you to prove beyond a shadow of a doubt that he is not tied to the Syndicate, or being used as a pawn in their twisted plan. For all of our own peace-of-mind."

Joey shook her head and gave him a confused look. "I don't know how much I can find that hasn't already been dug up. The man went through the Vice-Presidential security scan, not to mention the media hounds trying to find even the hint of dirt. What am I supposed to look for?"

Will leaned forward. "Everything," he said firmly. "Those other checks weren't looking for Syndicate ties. They wouldn't have even recognized them if they saw them. But you will."

It wasn't unusual for Will to be passionate about something, but his fierce explanation of her mission was a bit over-the-top, even for him.

It made sense to her though. If he was going to be leading a team on a clandestine operation at the request of the man, Will needed to trust him. Will trusted Ross and Flint, but he wasn't going to take their word for it.

"Can you do this, Joey?"

She nodded once. "I've got you, Gilbert. If there is anything suspicious about Harrison Coulter, I'll find it."

Will smiled tightly. "Thank you. Oh, and don't mention this to anyone else, okay?"

She hesitated, and then nodded. It wouldn't hurt to run the deep dive. Ross wouldn't like it, but if worse came to worst, he'd say that Coulter had nothing to hide.

Will left and Joey stood in the alcove alone for a minute, her mind racing with what had just transpired. Her phone buzzed, and she saw Cole's name flash. She took a deep breath. Instead of answering the call, she walked down the hall to the lobby.

Cole looked up with a grin. "Hey, I was just trying to call you."

"Yeah, I saw it." She hesitated. "Can we talk?"

# CHAPTER NINETEEN

"WHAT'S SO IMPORTANT?" Cole demanded after she explained that she'd be stuck here for the foreseeable future, tied up with something else.

"I can't tell you that," Joey said again.

He squeezed his fist, fighting the urge to pound it on the wall behind him. "So what? We're just done? The CPB-PGI project just dies because something else is more important?"

Joey's expression was sympathetic, but he didn't want sympathy. He wanted action. "We're so close. We just need a couple days!"

Her hand came to his arm. "I know. And I'll be here. I'm not abandoning you. I'll monitor the trap door from here at BTS and we'll catch them. But I can't be inside, out of reach. This other job is going to move quickly, and my team will need me."

Cole sagged. "What if I need you?" He whispered the question, aware of how pathetic he must have sounded. It wasn't just that he was desperate for her to help save the project. He wanted to be near her. To know that she was on the fourth floor at Zia or sleeping safely in his guest room.

Joey tipped her head up and lifted to her toes, kissing him gently. It soothed the anger slightly. "I'm sorry about the timing. I'll be here. We'll get him. And this other job will resolve and things will go back to normal."

Cole frowned. "That's the thing. This is our normal, isn't it?"

She tipped her head to the left, then the right. "Sometimes, yeah."

He sighed. "How can I hold that against you when I know eventually it will be me doing the same thing? It's why relationships never seem to work for me. I've never been on the receiving end of it though. It kind of sucks," he added bluntly.

Joey smiled. "After it's over, I'll tell you all about this other mission. And I hope you'll understand."

Cole nodded. "It's a date." He kissed her again. "Do we get to do dinner tonight?"

Joey shook her head slowly. "I wish, and not just because I'm starving. But I can't. I'll be camped out here until this mission is over."

Cole raised his eyebrows. "Camped out?"

"Yeah, we've got some beds for when we need to crash. But I've got some major work to do while we wait for your mole to trigger our trap. I'm just a call away, okay?"

"Take care of yourself."

———

Thirty minutes after Cole left, the first delivery arrived. The note stapled to the bag said "Don't forget to eat."

Garlic and basil wafted through the room as she opened the bag from Napoli's with a grin. The memory of her first dinner with Cole replayed as she looked around her office. It was the first time she'd truly seen the person behind the CEO suit. The man who would bring her dinner and wipe spilled lettuce off the floor. And he was still sending her food.

Joey ate the alfredo immediately, occasionally pausing to refresh the search algorithm. She was taking care of Will's request first. Then she'd need to set up the required security measures for worming her way into the FBI systems. Whatever Flint said about her ability, it wasn't going to be easy.

She sent a text to Cole while the algorithm dug through Coulter's personal bank transactions.

Joey: Thanks for dinner. Wish we could eat it together.

His response came almost immediately.

Cole: Me too. Maybe next time.

She smiled broadly and hit the video camera icon in the upper right. When he answered, it was obvious Cole was home.

"Well, hello there, beautiful. Isn't technology great?" he said.

She nodded and propped the phone up on her desk, blushing at the compliment. "It's not like being there, but at least I don't have to eat alone."

Cole smiled. "I'm glad. How are things going?"

She shrugged and took a bite. "Fine so far. Things are tense around here, but we're waiting for some intel before we can move."

"You sure you can't tell me?"

She rolled her eyes at him. "I'm definitely sure. But it's okay. We'll just have to talk about something else. Tell me about your family. Growing up."

She saw Cole hesitate and wondered if she had chosen a bad subject.

"I'm surprised you don't know it all already." His words held no bite, and the teasing tone made her smile.

"You're a surprisingly difficult man to dig up information on, Mr. Kensington."

"Tell me what you know, and I'll fill in the gaps."

"Okay, well… You grew up in Maryland. Your parents worked for the State Department and traveled extensively. I couldn't find anything about where you attended school, so I assume you were homeschooled while you traveled with them."

Cole shook his head. "Good guess, but no. My parents did work for State and they did travel a lot. But… I guess they didn't want to take me with them. I lived with my grandparents. And yes, they did homeschool me."

"Ahh, see. So close."

He smiled and raised his glass to her. "Yep. I'm sure you discovered that my parents died in a plane crash when I was fourteen. My grandfather started dealing with dementia years before that though."

More pieces of the Cole Kensington puzzle started to click into place in her mind. "That must have been really hard."

Cole nodded, but he was no longer looking at her through the phone. He was lost in a memory somewhere. "It was. My grandma tried her best, but she couldn't take care of him. He… became a different person. This kind, gentle hero of my mine slowly became an angry and vindictive stranger. Grandma cried all the time. And I just tried to be there, for both of them, you know? She died first, when I was seventeen. Grandpa was in a home by then."

Her heart broke for the young man he'd been back then, trying to hold the weight of the world on his shoulders, then landing in a group home. "I'm so sorry, Cole."

He looked back to her, as though remembering she were there for the first time. "I can't know for sure if my dad would have eventually had it too. As far as I know, he was still healthy when he died. But I never want to put anyone through what my grandma had to endure."

"You won't," she said automatically.

He clicked his tongue. "You don't know that, Joey. There's a genetic component to the disease. I might be slowly losing my memory and not even realize it. Every time I misplace something, the question is there, taunting me. Am I just human? Or am I getting old enough to start seeing the beginning stages?"

Joey didn't know what to say. "So what? You

want to get your vaccine approved so you can take it?"

He laughed. "Well, I wouldn't turn it down if we find out it works. I'd sign up for the first trials if I could somehow guarantee I wouldn't be in the placebo group. But no… I'm not actually optimistic enough to think we'll have that kind of breakthrough before it's too late for me."

"You might though, right? If we can stop whoever is trying to sabotage this gene therapy?"

He shrugged. "Maybe."

Joey finished the last of her dinner. "Well, I guess I better get to work then."

"Sorry, I didn't mean to be a buzzkill on this call."

She shook her head. "No, it was good. I like knowing more about you and why you are the man I know today. Sometime, I'd like to hear your side of the Jared story. He told me pieces."

Cole smiled warmly. "Oh, yeah… That's a pretty good story. Another time, I suppose."

"Take care of yourself."

"Back at you."

# CHAPTER TWENTY

A LAWYER COLE had never seen before met him at the police station and climbed into the back of the town car with him. "Hi, Mr. Kensington. Phillip Bankston. I'm a senior partner from Presley, Fisher, and Caldwell. I've been assigned your case."

"Where's Constance?" he asked, referring to the lawyer he usually dealt with from the firm.

"Constance is a contract attorney, Mr. Kensington. Right now, you are in need of a criminal defense attorney." Cole's gut churned as Bankston blathered on. "Now, your retainer with our firm covers all legal matters, and I'll walk through this with you every step of the way."

"I appreciate that. Thank you for coming."

Bankston nodded and waved a hand. "It's my job.

Now, when we go in there, don't say anything without checking with me. You know that, right? They claim you're just here for further questioning, but I've got word from the DA's office that they want you for this. They feel like they've got a solid case and are planning to pursue you as the killer."

Cole shook his head. "This is crazy. I would never hurt Laura."

At least not intentionally. Getting her involved in the search for the saboteur had been a mistake, one he'd regretted every minute since he'd done it. But that didn't make him the killer. He heard Joey's reassurances in his mind.

"I know that. You know that. Jared up there knows that," his lawyer said with a nod toward the driver's seat. "But these guys can only see the surface. And on the surface? It looks bad, Mr. Kensington."

Yeah, that sounded about right. Unfortunately, it was a lot easier and more fun to pin the murder inside the pharmaceutical company on the man who knew the victim and was there covered in her blood when the police arrived. Just like Joey had assumed he was part of the Syndicate just because he was rich, others were inclined to believe the same—that he would do whatever it took to get ahead. Including kill his friend.

His stomach roiled at the thought. If he were arrested, Laura's husband and children would see it. Would they believe that he had done such a thing?

He told Bankston about the suspected corporate espionage taking place at Zia, and how Laura had recently been brought in as a part of the investigation. Bankston nodded along. "If it seems like we need to, we'll tell the police about it. I'll tell you when. Otherwise, nothing."

"So what? We just go in there and don't say anything?"

"Yep. You can confirm anything that you already told them the night of the murder. But if they read you your rights, you're not saying another word. Got it?"

Cole blew out a breath. "Yeah, got it.'

"Okay, let's go."

"Just a sec." He pulled out his phone and sent a message to Joey. She needed to know what was going on. And why she might not get dinner delivered tonight. He hesitated though. He didn't want to send that message. It made it a bit too real. "Jared, can you make sure Joey gets dinner tonight if I'm held up here for some reason?"

His driver gave a small salute. "You got it. Food for Joey. Done."

"Thanks." With a deep breath, Cole stepped out of the car.

He was unsurprised when the detective's further questions turned into an interrogation. It helped to have his lawyer sitting next to him in the windowless room. And that he wasn't shaky with adrenaline and guilt like he had been Friday night.

"You're telling me you just happened to be meeting Ms. Conwell late on a Friday night and be the one to discover her body shortly after the murder?"

Cole bit the inside of his cheek. He turned to his lawyer for permission, who nodded. Cole turned back to the detective. "Yes. Laura requested we meet."

"What was the meeting about?"

"That's confidential," he replied.

"Mr. Kensington, might I remind you that we are trying to solve a murder?"

"We both know the purpose of Mr. Kensington's meeting with one of the lead researchers within his company has no bearing on the murder investigation, unless you believe he is the killer." His lawyer's quick response niggled at Cole's conscience.

"It would help clear his name if we knew why

they were meeting so late at night," the detective offered.

Cole leaned over to whisper, "Should I tell them about the mole?"

His lawyer hesitated, then nodded. Cole turned and met the steely-faced detective's eyes. "This is strictly confidential. Earlier this week, I informed Laura that I suspected a mole inside her team who was leaking information and potentially sabotaging results. She requested this meeting to discuss something she had discovered. Unfortunately, I don't know what it might have been."

The detective sneered. "Well, isn't that convenient?"

Cole rolled his head back. "Oh come on. You can't think I made up an entire security breach to cover my own tracks."

The detective sneered at him. "That's exactly what I think. I'm not going to let you get away with this, Mr. Kensington. All you rich shmucks are the same. Just because you've got money and a high-priced lawyer, you think you can do whatever you want." He jabbed a meaty finger into the table. "But it's not happening on my watch. To clarify, Mr. Kensington, you're under arrest for the murder of Laura Conwell."

Cole stammered his objections. Was this guy serious? The detective continued to recite his rights in a monotone voice. Bankston placed his hand on Cole's arm.

"This is absurd, detective. Mr. Kensington is willing to answer your questions to help you find the real killer."

"Well, I'm pretty sure we've already got the real killer. Now, I'm going to ask some more questions, and Mr. Kensington here is welcome to tell me what he says really happened. Why don't you tell me about your accomplice. I'm sure we'll be bringing her in soon. Miss Rodriguez, was it?"

Cole jerked away from the table, his blood running hot. "No!" It was one thing to go after him. But he wouldn't let them drag Joey into this. She hadn't done anything.

————

Dolores's husky voice came through the phone when Joey picked it up on the second ring.

"There is a very nice-looking man here with some food for you. He'd like a chance to talk."

Joey smiled reflexively. "I'll be right there." She

hadn't seen nearly enough of Cole in person since the day the President was shot.

She smoothed a hand over her hair and hurried down the hallway toward the lobby. She stopped short when she opened the door and saw Jared sitting there, instead of Cole. Disappointment crashed over her.

"Oh. Jared, I wasn't expecting you."

He gave a smile, but it quickly disappeared. "Sorry to disappoint, ma'am."

She shook her head. "No, it's fine. I just thought… Dolores said…" She waved her hand. "It doesn't matter. What's with the personal delivery?"

Jared looked around the open lobby. "Is there someplace better we can talk?"

Joey ushered him into the conference room and shut the door. The solemn expression on Jared's face hadn't faded. "What's going on? Where's Cole?"

"Well, that's why I'm here. He needs your help, Joey. The police brought him in for questioning this afternoon, and then they arrested him for Laura's murder. His lawyer reached out to me. Apparently, they want you for it, too."

Joey shut her eyes in frustration. What a nightmare. She couldn't let that happen. She had to find this guy before things got even worse. And, of course, she was still trying to do what she needed to on Operation Blue Smoke. She needed help.

"Well, that's not great. Thanks, Jared."

"Joey!" The call came from the back hallway.

With an apologetic look to Jared, she said, "I'm so sorry, I've got to go. I'll be in touch."

With that, she headed back to the part of BTS Headquarters that existed behind the security doors, letting them close firmly behind her.

———

Cole sat in the holding area outside the commissioner's office, staring at his feet. Somehow, his lawyer had managed to sneak them inside the building. The news of his arrest had made it to the media, and he wasn't looking forward to his mugshot being on the front page. Which it would be, no doubt.

He looked up when someone called to him from the side of the room. Jared waved at him, and he made his way over. "Anything?"

He'd been desperate for word from Joey for the last twenty-four hours. Scenarios of her in handcuffs had been haunting him last night in his jail cell—an experience he never thought he'd share with Jared, but here he was.

"I'm sorry, man. She barely came out to see me when I stopped by to tell her about you. I haven't heard a word since."

Cole felt his heart sink. His only hope had been that somehow Joey would stand by him through all this. Maybe even figure out how to prove his innocence.

But she was too busy for him.

His lawyer joined the conversation with a word-less nod to Jared. Then he turned to Cole. "We were supposed to meet with Commissioner Davis, but there was a last-minute change of schedule. We're on the docket for Commissioner O'Hara at nine thirty."

Cole frowned. "Do you know why the change?"

His lawyer shrugged and shook his head. "No idea, but I'm not looking a gift horse in the mouth. Davis is notoriously tough on defendants up for murder. We've got a much better shot with O'Hara."

Well, that was good news. He said a quick prayer of thanks for that small blessing. However it worked out, he wasn't going to stop seeing God's hand in this crazy situation.

He saw a woman down the hall. Was she looking at him? Her big sunglasses made it hard to tell. She tipped them down and Cole gasped. His lawyer turned to him, "What's wrong?"

"I, uh, need to use the restroom."

"Officer, my client would like to use the facilities. Can someone escort him?"

———

Joey listened to Cole's excuse through the listening device she'd slipped on his attorney's lapel. She ducked into the men's room.

A few moments later, Cole came inside. "What are you doing here? You can't be here! They're still looking for you," he whispered his concerns, but she silenced them by pressing her lips against his.

"I'm so sorry this is happening, Cole. Jared came and told me and I just—"

Cole kissed her again, then pulled away. "You shouldn't have come."

Joey shook her head. "I'll be just fine, don't worry about me. Besides, someone had to make sure you got a good judge for your bail hearing."

Cole paused, then smiled. "You did that?"

She nodded. "It's not a guarantee or anything. I just hope it's enough. From what I pulled of court records, O'Hara is the most defendant-friendly when it comes to setting bail. I'm just hoping she doesn't hold your fortune against you."

Cole touched her cheek, and she savored the contact. "Like you do?"

"Like I used to," she corrected him.

He stared into her eyes. "Thank you," he said. "What about your other job? The big top-secret one? Don't you need to be working on that?"

She nodded but grabbed his hand and squeezed. "This was more important. I called in some reinforcements for the other thing. You and I? We'll get to the bottom of this. As soon as you're out on bail, Jared will be waiting outside, and you can come be with me at BTS."

"Sounds like heaven," he responded.

A bang on the door interrupted their embrace. Cole turned and yelled, "I'll be right out."

His eyes met hers again. "I'll see you soon, okay? Stay safe. And if I don't get out… don't worry about me. Just take care of yourself."

Tears flooded her eyes and she shook her head. "No way. We're a team."

He leaned down and kissed her once more. "I love you, Joey."

Her eyes flew open and she watched helplessly as he stepped out of the stall. She wanted to respond, but she was speechless. Love? Was it too soon? Maybe he was just saying that because he was soon to be on trial for murder.

She shook her head. There was no way.

Cole Kensington?

She buried her face in her hands and held back the laughter.

"Hello? Is someone in here?" The deep voice came from the stall next to hers.

She lifted her head. Ooops.

"Oh dear," she exclaimed in an exaggerated southern accent. "I thought this was the little girls' room!"

Then she rushed out the door and left the court-house, praying desperately for Cole's hearing.

# CHAPTER
## TWENTY-ONE

"YOUR HONOR, the district attorney's office requests no provision for bail. The brutal murder of Laura Conwell must be dealt with strictly. Furthermore, this man is one of the richest in America with no familial ties. He has the means to post even the highest bail without hardship."

Cole held perfectly still, despite the way he wanted to jump up and argue just why everything the district attorney said was complete nonsense. He'd never leave, even if it meant going to jail. While it still seemed completely impossible, he knew it wasn't. The detective seemed so sure of himself, and Cole couldn't figure out why. The worst part was that they thought Joey had something to do with the whole thing.

"My client is an upstanding member of society, with a business and a charitable foundation to his name that he would never dream of leaving behind. He maintains his innocence and has cooperated with the police at every step of the process, despite their hostility toward him. Mr. Kensington has obligations to fulfill that cannot be dealt with from behind bars. He is also willing to relinquish his passport as a sign of good faith if it would please the court."

Cole took a deep breath. It seemed that Bankston was worth every penny of the very fat retainer he'd already been paid.

"I see the point the district attorney is trying to make," the commissioner started, and Cole's heart sank. "But I have to agree with Mr. Kensington's lawyer. There is no reason to believe he is a flight risk. That being said, I'd like to give him a strong incentive to return to court at the appointed time. Bail is set at ten million dollars." The gavel hit the sound block.

Cole jolted at the sound. Following the back-and-forth interplay of arguments between the lawyers had been fascinating and anxiety inducing. For a moment, he'd been sure he was going to spend the next several months in custody, waiting for the trial and helpless to do anything to clear his name.

Bankston clapped him on the shoulder. "Let's get the paperwork done and get you home, Mr. Kensington."

Cole smiled. "Thank you. I really appreciate it."

"Don't thank me. Thank your little friend with the hookup in the court system."

Cole raised his eyebrows. "I'm sure I don't know what you're talking about."

Bankston nodded. "If you say so. But a friend in the clerk's office told me that schedules don't just change like this unless someone pulls some major strings. It would seem you've got friends in high places, Mr. Kensington."

Cole smiled as Bankston led the way to the commissioner's office where he would fill out the bond paperwork and get the money wired. He wasn't sure he'd call Joey's dark computer cave "high places," but he was sure glad she was his friend.

And more.

He groaned at the way he'd admitted his feelings for her. In a bathroom stall, while she was wearing a ridiculous disguise to avoid getting arrested. What was he thinking?

He hadn't been, to be honest. He'd been so grateful to see her and hold her and that she had set aside her other important work to focus on him. So

much emotion had welled up inside him, and he
didn't know how else to express it.

He loved her.

And now he just had to clear his name, catch the
culprit, and save his company. No sweat.

When he left the courthouse, a handful of
reporters waited to ambush him. They hurled questions at him, rapid-fire, without waiting for a response
before asking another.

"Mr. Kensington, did you murder Laura
Conwell?"

"Were you lovers?"

Cole stumbled, appalled at the question.

"Was she blackmailing you?"

"Cole, don't." His lawyer's words were firm and
probably wise, but Cole couldn't ignore it.

He held up his hand to silence the torrent of
questions.

"I'll be giving a longer formal statement later. For
now, I'll say this." He looked squarely into one of the
cameras trained on him. "I had nothing to do with the
death of Laura Conwell. I'm hurting at the loss of my
dear friend, and my heart breaks for her husband and
children, all of whom I know personally. Please know
that any implication that Laura was involved with
something unsavory is unequivocally false. I will

fight in court to maintain my innocence, and I will do everything in my power to make sure the real killer is brought to justice."

With that, he ignored the additional questions yelled at him and strode toward Jared, who was waiting for him at the car. Bankston climbed in after him.

The door closed and Bankston chuckled. "I forget what it's like to have clients who know what to say and how to say it. You nailed that."

Cole waved a hand. "It was the truth. I couldn't let them say those things about Laura. She was innocent in all this."

As much as Cole wanted to go directly to BTS Headquarters to see Joey, he knew he had some things to take care of first. After dropping Bankston off at his office, he called her instead.

"Hey, beautiful." He couldn't fight the grin on his face and the light tone of his words.

"Oh, I'm so glad to hear your voice!" she said by way of greeting.

"I guess you heard the news?"

"I was listening," she said.

"What?" he laughed. "How?"

"Well, I *ran into* Mr. Bankston this morning at the courthouse and left a little something to give me ears inside the courtroom. He's very good at his job, I'd say."

Cole smiled and settled into the seat. "And you are very good at yours, Miss Rodriguez." That was the understatement of the century. She was scary talented. At least she used her powers for good.

"I miss you. Are you coming here?" Her words filled him with longing to hold her again, mixed with a bit of satisfaction that she was so eager to do the same.

He sighed. "I will. I want to, but I really need to show my face at the office and run some damage control."

She didn't answer for a moment. Cole wished he had a listening device that let him listen to her thoughts as easily as she listened to court this morning.

"Joey?"

"I'm here. Yeah, I totally understand." She sounded distracted and a bit sad. "I'll be here when you get here."

"Any nibbles on our trap?"

"Nothing yet," she said.

"Okay. Keep me posted."

He hung up, slightly dissatisfied about the way the call ended. Everything in him ached to go see Joey and celebrate his freedom—however temporary it might be. For the first time in as long as he could remember, he wanted to put something ahead of his company. He still had to go to Zia right now, but it was kind of a big deal that he actually wished he could do something else.

He'd put his company ahead of relationships before. But he'd never felt regret or disappointment because of having to make that choice.

It was just another indication that something was different about Joey and his feelings for her.

He had a sneaking suspicion that even if he lost everything and ended up in prison, he'd still be okay if Joey would stay by his side. Which was crazy, because what woman would stand beside a convicted murderer, even if she knew he was innocent?

Somehow, though, he knew that Joey would.

# CHAPTER TWENTY-TWO

JOEY ROLLED her eyes and looked to Steven for sympathy. The phone on her desk was on speaker with Will Gilbert from his place in the field.

"Will, you're not listening. I can't just hack into someone's computer from here. It has to be connected to a network, *or* I have to physically have access. Otherwise, there is no way in. Who is this woman, anyway? What does she have to do with Blue Smoke?"

"It's a long story. But she's here now, and I need to know what she knows."

"So ask her," she said. "But unless there is a way in, I can't give you anything. Get access to the computer and then we can talk."

"Fine. Thanks for nothing, Joey."

"Always a pleasure, Will."

The phone disconnected, and Joey turned back to Steven. "Where were we?" She'd reached out to Steven, who she'd only known online as Vertigo. She'd connected with him through a few of the hacker chat rooms she still frequented. She hadn't expected the scrawny nineteen-year-old who'd shown up, but who was she to judge? From everything she'd seen from him, Vertigo was a talented hacker. And, more importantly, was a genuinely good person who had learned hacking for the thrill of learning. Not to cause chaos.

Steven shook his head. "What? Sorry. I just can't believe I'm here with Phoenix. Like, in real life. This is crazy. I'm geeking out right now."

She chuckled. "I'm pretty excited to be here with Vertigo. But here, please call me Joey."

Steven nodded. "Oh, right. Joey. Umm, we were pulling the NSA satellite images," he said with a bewildered shake of his head. "I can't believe that sentence just came out of my mouth."

She chuckled. "Oh, that's right. It's all good. It'll take some getting used to. Trust me, this isn't my usual network either. Will wants as much information about the shooter as possible. We're going to see if the NSA knows anything we don't."

An alert sounded from a program in the background of her screen, and Joey's heart leapt. It was the trap door inside Zia's server.

"What's that?" Steven's question made her stop just before she clicked into it and changed programs.

"It's another project. You take lead on the NSA server. Dig as much as you can and see what you can get to Gilbert. Don't forget to mask your access like we talked about. You should be in the clear from here."

Steven nodded. "Okay, cool. I'm on it."

Joey loved the confidence. She knew Steven was the right choice for this.

She grabbed her laptop and jogged to the conference room, pulling up the program as she went. She apologized as Flint dodged her in the hallway.

Setting the laptop down, she pulled out her phone to call Cole. "Come on, pick up," she pleaded to the ringing phone.

There was no answer, so she left a message. "Cole, it's me. We've got a bite. Call me back."

Joey watched through her system as the mole accessed the altered files. She dialed Cole again, but again, no answer.

"Drat. We should have been set up at Zia. What was I thinking?"

If they'd had a team onsite right now, she could have pinpointed the location where the files were being accessed, and the team could get the man right then and there. But with Zia headquarters being all the way on the other side of DC in Maryland, there was no way Black Tower could get there. And Zia security wasn't exactly up for the job of facing down a killer.

As it was, it was all going to depend on the little bit of code she'd hidden in the fake reports. She said a quick prayer. All she could do was watch and wait for her program to send up the signal.

Cole called her back thirty minutes later.

"I'm sorry," he started. "Did we miss him?"

She clicked her tongue. "Yeah, unfortunately. I could see him pulling the files from the lab computer, but he's not in there anymore as far as I can tell."

"What now?" Cole asked. "Was that it? Why weren't we ready?" His agitation was clear.

"Hey, hey. Calm down. We're okay. He might have the files, but he also took a little present with them. It'll ping us every thirty minutes, as long as the device is connected to a network."

Cole was silent for a moment, and Joey winced. She thought her little trick was good, but maybe she should have checked with Cole about the right tactic to–

"That's brilliant. You can do that?"

Her smile grew wide. "You sure ask me that a lot," she said, thinking of their first meeting.

"You'd think I'd have learned by now," he agreed.

"I think you'd know I'm the *best by* now," she teased.

His chuckle was low, and a thrill ran through her chest. "Can I see you tonight?" he asked.

"I'll be here," she confirmed. "We've got a lot going on in the other operation, but I'll be watching my little Hansel and Gretel bug send me bread-crumbs. When we have a team ready, we'll get Flint to approve a strike team."

"I can't believe we might really get him." The bewilderment in his voice let her know where his thoughts were. Capturing the culprit would fix every-thing. The therapy project timeline, the trial for Laura's death, her hiding out under protection. All of it could finally come to an end when they had him in custody.

"We'll get him," she said firmly. "You can trust my guys."

"That's what Flint is always telling me. That's

what he told me about you, and that turned out all right."

She twirled in the conference room chair with a smile on her face. The exhilaration of the spinning was nothing compared to the euphoria she felt when Cole Kensington reaffirmed his affection for her.

————

Once again, Cole sat next to Joey in her office cave, illuminated by the screens surrounding them. Flint stood behind them, arms crossed and his eyes on the screen. She wore a headset, but they could all hear the audio from the strike team.

Cole had met each man before they headed out in an armored SUV. He knew Ryder from hanging out with Flint. Marshall and Jackson Kelley were new faces to him, but the brothers seemed competent, though completely different than one another. Jackson was a typical showoff personality—Cole had come across far too many of them during his career. Marshall was more serious and focused. The fourth member of the team was Connor James. Joey said he was new but solid.

"Team Alpha is in position." It sounded like

Ryder, but Cole couldn't be sure. "You sure this is the place, Joey?"

She nodded, then answered audibly. "The signal has been pinging from this address for the last four hours—every thirty minutes, just as expected."

"Pretty nice house for a killer. Maybe we're in the wrong business." That was Jackson. Even Cole could figure that one out.

"Shut up, Jax. Team Bravo is in position."

"We should get another ping in one minute, boys. Then you can move in," Joey instructed the team.

Cole felt his heart rate tick up another notch. "What if he's not there?" he wondered out loud.

"He'll be there," she responded confidently.

Cole wasn't so sure. Just because the computer was there didn't mean that the culprit was.

"Here comes the ping," Joey said. "Three, two, one… Wait." She furrowed her brow. "I didn't get a signal."

"Hold your positions," Flint commanded, turning toward her. "Joey, what's going on?"

Her fingers were flying across the keyboard, her eyes intensely focused on the screens. "I don't know. Give me a minute." Her eyes widened and she leaned forward. "Sneaky son-of-a…" She didn't look away from the screens for a second as she talked. "He's on the offensive. He's tracing me back."

Cole sucked in a breath and watched, feeling helpless.

Flint was as intense as Cole had ever seen him. "What about the team? Do I need to abort?"

She shook her head. "Just give me a minute."

"There's movement inside the house," Ryder gave the update with a far calmer voice than Cole would have.

"Hold on! I've almost got him."

Cole watched, amazed at her ability to take in information on the screens so quickly.

"Come on… where are you?" Joey whispered to herself as she worked. Cole jumped when she suddenly yelled. "Abort, abort! It's a trap. Don't move in."

"Forget that. We can take a nerdy computer guy. I'm going in." There was Jackson again.

"He's not there!" Joey's desperate yell cut through Cole like a knife.

"Jackson, don't—" Flint's command was cut off by a muffled yell on the other end of the line.

# CHAPTER TWENTY-THREE

INSIDE HER OFFICE, everything went silent as they waited for an update.

"Team Bravo is holding position. Even if one of us still can't follow orders." Marshall's voice was full of irritation, and Joey relaxed into her chair knowing that no one had walked into danger.

Ryder's calm voice came over the speaker. "Eagle, can you repeat your last?"

She leaned into the mic. "I said, he's not there. I've got his location. He's back inside Zia."

"Are you sure?" Cole's question came from her right and she turned. His warm eyes watched her, full of trust.

"Absolutely," she nodded. "I don't know what he left inside that house, but I don't think we want to find out. "He must have found my beacon bug and set a trap. But I got him trying to dig his way back into our system."

"Why would he go back to Zia though?"

She shook her head. "I don't really know… But that's where he is. I'm sure of it." She'd gotten him, in real time with no ability to hide behind fancy firewalls or spoofed locations. She didn't know why, but their mysterious hacker was back at Zia.

She turned to Flint. "Do you trust me?"

Flint tipped his head back and forth. "I don't know, Joey. That seems unlikely. I'm with Cole, why would he go back there?"

Frustrated with her boss, she turned to Cole. "Well? It's your company. Your project. What do you want to do?"

Cole's eyes flicked between her and Flint, then back again. He gave a sharp nod. "We trust Joey. She got us this far. Let's go to Zia and nail this guy."

Relief and pride filled her at his words of confidence.

"Will he know we're coming?" Flint asked.

Joey shook her head. "I don't think so. But we need to hurry. He's stonewalled for now, but he's very good." Surprisingly good, she realized. This was no research assistant selling secrets. From the security logs and the detection of the beacon bug, there was no doubt in her mind that this was an experienced hacker.

Did she know them?

After all, it was a small circle.

She sent a message to Vertigo.

**I need a favor. Cross-reference current Zia employees with previous Raven Tech employees or contractors.**

"What should we do about the house?" Ryder's voice came across the line, tinged with frustration and impatience.

She chuckled. "Sorry, boys. Change of plans. You need to head to Zia Pharmaceuticals. Be discreet."

"Aww, man. Do you know what a letdown it is to make it to T minus five seconds and then call it all off? It's like having the bases loaded in the bottom of the ninth to win the game and then the star strikes out. Total letdown."

"Game's not over yet, Jax. Stop being so dramatic." Joey smiled at Marshall's words to his younger brother.

"Let's go," Cole said.

She turned to him. "What? No way. You're not going. That guy tried to kill us!"

Cole frowned. "I'm going. That's my company.

I'm sick and tired of this guy running circles around me and my security team. I'm going so I can have the satisfaction of seeing him walked out in handcuffs."

Joey turned to Flint. "You can't possibly be okay with this."

Flint shrugged. "It's his property. What would you have me do? Besides, our guys will need him to get access."

Joey looked back and forth between her two favorite people in the world. Cole's expression was determined, but his eyes zeroed in on her. "I need to do this, Joey."

She chewed the inside of her cheek as she considered. "Fine, but I'm coming too. We better get moving."

Cole's eyes widened. "What?"

"There's no way I'm sitting here and watching from a distance. Especially with your Fort Knox security and signal blocking. Unless I'm inside Zia, I'll be blind. So, let's go."

On the ride, Joey pulled out her laptop and went back through the tracks the hacker had left behind while trying to infiltrate BTS. She knew this signature; she just needed to remember from where. It almost reminded her of….

"Hey, Flint. Do you know whatever happened…

to StormHunter?" Even saying the name of one of her former allies was difficult. Storm had been the mastermind of the hack that landed her in federal custody and onto Flint's radar. Flint wasn't a hacker himself, but his network was far deeper than anyone typically realized.

"I never heard anything else about him after the team fell apart. Rumor had it that a big portion of The Alliance were ticked at him for selling you out."

Joey let that sink in. She'd resisted digging for more information for years. It hurt so badly to have been betrayed by Storm. His last comments before her arrest still stuck in her mind.

StormHunter: We're all just cogs in a giant machine. And sometimes, we get sacrificed for the greater good.

"Do you think it's him?" Flint asked.

Joey stared at the code. If this was StormHunter, after all these years... It would explain the talent level, though not how he'd hacked the Raven Tech system. Unless he'd worked there too, and she'd never made the connection. He could have paid someone else. Another cog in his stupid machine.

"I don't know," she answered honestly. "Could be. But I don't know who he is or what he looks like. I would have never thought he was a killer. But it was a long time ago."

If this was StormHunter, did he know he was up against her? He'd never known her real name. Just her online handle. Alantara. After her arrest, Alantara had disappeared from the black hat hacker world. And Phoenix had appeared. Rescued from the ashes of betrayal and hurt… and brought back to a new life in Christ, with a new purpose.

When they reached Zia, Joey tucked her bag under her arm. She held Cole's hand as they strode across the sidewalk in the dark. The BTS team was already waiting in the security office.

She set up her computer, plugging directly into the Zia network and remotely accessing the BTS server. She zeroed in on the hacker's location. There was no employee identified on the access logs, but at least she knew where he was, if not who.

"He's still here." She looked up at Cole. "He's desperate. And we don't have much time. He's grabbing the data from every file he can get his hands on. The lab. Basement level two."

Cole's face went pale. "We've got to stop him."

Flint pointed to Jackson and Ryder. "Take the east steps." Then to Marshall and Connor, "You two take the west. Joey, make sure they have access."

She nodded. "Unlocking everything now."

"You can't do that, ma'am," came the timid voice

of the security guard whose office they were intruding on.

The four men in tactical gear straightened and stepped forward. Cole held up a hand. "Yes, as a matter of fact, she can."

Flint rolled his eyes and pointed to Ryder, Jackson, Marshall, and Connor. "Go on, get moving. Stay on comms."

Joey smiled and returned to her keyboard, quickly disengaging the locks on the staircases. She slipped an earbud out of the case and stuck it in her ear, passing another to Cole, so he could listen to the operation as well.

Within the Raven Tech security system RT800X she watched for any movement. StormHunter, or whoever it was, was still in the basement, as far as she could tell.

"We're in the basement," came the call over the comms. "What are we looking for?"

"Anyone," she replied snarkily. "It's eleven at night. Pretty much anyone here is up to no good."

"Geez, how many rats are in this place? They're so gross."

Joey rolled her eyes. "It's medical research, Jackson. Put on your big girl panties."

A flag on the security map caught her attention. "He's on the fourth floor. Move!"

"On our way," came the reply from Ryder.

The locks re-engaged on the basement stairwells. Her guys were trapped. Joey tried to unlock them but pounded the table in frustration.

"Joey, the doors won't open." The team in the basement had just realized the same thing she had.

"I know! Give me a second." She tried again to no avail. The hacker had trapped them, and she couldn't override the control for a second time. "I can't get them out!" There was desperation in her voice as she turned to Flint for support.

He only shook his head. "What do we know?"

She zeroed in on the server room. That's where he was going.

If she couldn't unlock the basement doors, she could at least prevent him from adjusting anything else. She activated a total system freeze. Even Storm-Hunter wouldn't be able to undo that. Which meant they could get him on the fourth floor.

Her phone buzzed, and she saw the short message from Vertigo.

**Ben Parker worked at Raven Tech for six months three years ago.**

Ben was StormHunter? That was crazy. It had

been ten years since she'd worked with him in the Alliance. Wasn't he too young? Maybe she was seeing ghosts where there weren't any. Just because StormHunter had the skills didn't mean that he was the one targeting Cole's company.

Ben had the means and the opportunity. If he knew the RT800x system the way she did, he was the one who'd been using that skill to duck around the server and the building without being caught. And he was the one on the fourth floor server room right now.

She started toward the door. "Let's go."

"What? Are you crazy? What about Ryder and the team?"

"I can get them out later when I have more time. But right now, we've got to go stop him from dumping the entire server." She pointed to the security guards. "Move!"

Flint sighed. "You're right. Let's go." He looked at Cole. "You have some weapons around here?"

Cole nodded and pointed to another door. "In there. Joey, are you sure you should—"

"I'm fully trained, Cole. Let's get this guy."

After they all had weapons, Flint took charge. "Cole, Joey, and Robbie here take the east stairs. I'll go with Zach and the West. Stay on comms."

"Worst operation ever," came Jackson's snarky commentary from the basement.

"Be careful," was his brother Marshall's reply.

Joey silenced Jackson's line with a few keystrokes before she ducked back out of the room. "Thanks, Marshall. Watch your back down there."

"Ryder's got an idea. We'll see you upstairs if it works."

Joey raised her eyebrows. There was no way out of that basement, she was sure of it. But she'd learned never to underestimate Ryder and the team.

# CHAPTER
# TWENTY-FOUR

COLE FELT the heavy weight of the gun in his hand. The safety was on, and he wasn't entirely unfamiliar with the weapon, but the shooting range was entirely different than stalking up the stairs of his own company headquarters preparing to come face-to-face with the man who'd been sabotaging his projects for months.

He followed Joey up the stairs, meeting her glance on the landing between flights. "Hey, you sure you're okay?" he said. Hearing everything about Storm-Hunter and watching her battle this enemy through the computer. It was becoming personal for her, just like it was for him.

"I'm good. We're going to get him. This is it, right?"

Cole nodded. He sure hoped so. And he prayed it would be before this guy trashed all the servers and set Zia back decades in research and trials.

When they reached the 4th floor, Cole was regretting all those morning workouts he'd skipped in the last six months.

In his earpiece, Flint's voice came loud and clear. "We're at the landing. You guys here?"

Joey responded for them. "Ready."

"Breach on three," Flint commanded.

"One."

Cole adjusted his grip, his palms sweaty and his heart racing.

"Two."

His gaze flicked to Joey, who was focused entirely on the door in front of them. He knew she wanted to be here, and she was obviously capable, but he'd much prefer her to be safely tucked behind her computer.

"Three!"

At Flint's command, Joey pushed through the door, sweeping left. Robbie followed and moved right. Cole wasn't sure exactly what to do, but based on the hundred or so action movies he'd seen in the last decade, he held his gun out and pressed forward.

Joey whispered, "Move toward the server room.

Keep your eyes open because he might already be on the move."

Cole flinched at the sudden noise in front of him, then ducked as the wall behind him exploded. "Get down!" He scrambled to take cover behind one of the desks in the wide-open office space. Stupid open offices. Joey was right, this was a terrible concept for a workspace.

Where was Joey? He found her across the room, in a similar position as himself, huddled behind a filing cabinet.

"You won't make it out of here!" she yelled at the shooter.

There was a gunshot in response, striking the edge of the cabinet. Joey retreated a bit farther. Cole stuck his head up, trying to spot the shooter across the room. There was no sign of him.

"We've got this floor surrounded and more agents onsite!" Cole yelled. "If you turn yourself in, we can work something out."

He heard a chuckle and paused, zeroing in on where it was coming from.

"We're approaching from the east. Can you distract him?" Cole praised the Lord for his friend. Together, they could take him down.

Joey slowly peeked her head around the cabinet,

searching for the killer. Cole pointed toward the cubicle he thought the man was hiding in.

———

Joey kept her finger alongside the trigger as she crouched while making her way across the aisle, ducking from cubicle to cubicle.

"What's your endgame, anyway? There's no way out of this."

"You just let me worry about that."

Joey's breath caught at the voice. There was no denying it now.

On her comms, she whispered, "That's Ben Parker." Her mind raced, still trying to connect the dots. Despite Patrick assigning him to bring her up-to-speed in the department, Ben had been completely disengaged from the beginning. Had he known she was an imposter from the start?

She saw him emerge from his cubicle, ducking as he fired several rounds in their direction. Hundreds of pieces of glass rained down on her from the cubicle divider, stinging like a hundred papercuts as they hit her bare arms. When it was safe to look again, the door was closing to the server room.

What was he thinking? That was a total dead end.

"He's in the server room, Raven," she said. She had to get in there.

"I got him."

"Wait. It's a dead end. I don't understand. He's trapped. Why would he go in there?"

She stood and watched as Cole and Robbie did the same. Then Flint and Zach appeared from behind the desks across the room.

Cole growled in frustration. "It's gotta be a suicide mission. He's just trying to destroy as much as he can."

Joey shook her head. "No... I don't think so. He's got a way out. We just need to figure out what it is."

Ben ducked back out and ran across the office, firing wildly and forcing them all to take cover.

"I'm going for the server room!" If her estimate was correct, she only had a few minutes to stop the program that would wipe every file from the Zia mainframe. That's what he'd been doing in there.

"You guys go. I'll get him," came Flint's reply.

"We're on our way," she heard Ryder's update through her earpiece, a surge of victory rushing through her to accompany his words.

Ducking low, she crouched behind the row of desks closest to the wall and beelined it for the server room door. Cole followed closely behind.

With one final glance at the exchange of gunfire behind her between Flint and Ben, she ran to the server door and hurried inside.

"I wondered when you'd get here, Alantara."

————

Cole's heart froze as he recognized the man holding a gun on Joey.

"Patrick?"

"Cole. Nice of you to join us in this little reunion. Even if you weren't invited." Patrick's smile was twisted and mocking.

He shook his head, his mind refusing to accept the image in front of him. "I don't understand. You're my friend."

Patrick scoffed. "You don't know what friendship is, Cole."

"Are you… StormHunter?" Joey's voice was full of trepidation. He couldn't tell if it was fear from the gun currently pointed at her face or because of the history between them. What had Patrick called her? Alantara?

"StormHunter, Ibycus, Neo. They're all me."

Cole gaped at the man he thought he knew. Five years, and Patrick had him entirely convinced that he knew his way around a computer just enough to manage a team of tech staff. Apparently, that was all a sham.

In his earpiece came the comforting chatter of the rest of the team.

"Did we know there were two of them?"

"We're on the fourth floor. What's the situation, Raven?"

"I'm under fire, pinned down on the East wing."

"Roger. We're exiting the elevator in three, two, one."

Joey was still talking to Patrick, that same sad reflection in her voice. "I… I trusted you."

Patrick laughed. "And that was foolish, wasn't it? I always said you shouldn't trust anyone, Alantara."

"Her name is Joey!" Cole didn't like this. Any of it. Joey looked so vulnerable and broken right now. "Don't listen to him, Joey. You can trust the right people."

"Listen to him, talking about trust as though he sees people as anything more than pawns in his quest for greatness. You and I, Alantara, we were truly great together. We could have changed the world." He spoke with an affection that made Cole queasy. Patrick took a step toward Joey, and Cole lunged.

Patrick swung the gun around and the shot exploded. In the small space, the sound was everywhere, deafening and disorienting. Cole reached for his side as the sharp burning pain registered.

# CHAPTER
# TWENTY-FIVE

JOEY YELLED as Cole staggered backward and slumped against one of the server cabinets. Her ears were ringing, and her own voice sounded distant and detached. "Cole! Cole!"

She moved toward him, but an arm around her waist stopped her and held her firmly in place, despite her struggle as she tried to reach Cole. The hard pressure of the gun pushing into her ribcage made her stop fighting.

"Please, let me help him," she begged.

"Joey, hang on. We're on our way!"

"I'm disappointed in you, *Joey*," he sneered. "You know, I wondered what happened to you. When I heard the feds grabbed you, I was so disappointed. I really thought you had the chops to make it happen."

Joey faltered, wincing against the pressure of the gun to her side. "You let me take the fall for the entire Alliance. If it weren't for Flint, I'd have been left to rot in a cell. At least now I'm with people I can trust."

Patrick tsked. "You think you can trust them any more than you could trust me? After the Alliance fell apart, I landed at Parsenix. Keeping my head down like a good little hacker. Until your precious little billionaire over there bought us out. Look at him." He jerked his head toward Cole. "You trust a billionaire? He's the worst of the lot. He buys companies and tears them apart and for what? A few employees with a skillset he needs with no regard for the rest."

"Michelle," she breathed in sudden understanding. This was all about Michelle.

She cried out as he pulled her tighter and shoved the gun farther into her side.

"No! It's just like with you. You're nothing but a tool he needs to protect his precious drug money."

Joey shook her head. "No, you're wrong."

"When you showed up, I didn't know it was you at first. But then I saw that little gift you left in the files. You can't hide from me because I know who you really are. At least I never held you back. At least I pushed you to do whatever it took to make a difference in the world."

He scowled. "Flint Raven? Seriously?" Patrick spat the words. "You think he's some sort of savior, rescuing you from the clutches of the FBI? All you did was trade one jail sentence for another. You're a mindless drone, Joey, doing whatever someone else tells you to do. You can't trust anyone, Alantara."

Tears were streaming down her face at his accusations. His words were tiny daggers, aimed with precision to reveal deep doubts and insecurities she had buried.

"Joey, tell me what's going on!" Raven's voice crackled in her ear.

Cole groaned from his position huddled on the floor. "Don't listen, Joey," he rasped.

"Shut up, Kensington, or she gets a matching hole in her spleen."

Was he right? What made her think Flint was any different? Or Cole? Flint might have saved her from the FBI, but it was only so she could work at Raven Tech. And now at Black Tower.

And Cole would have never given her a second look if she hadn't been who he needed to protect his company. He couldn't possibly love her. The real her. Not Alantara. Not Phoenix.

Just Joey.

But his words and actions over the last few weeks

played out in her mind. His honesty. His thoughtfulness. His declaration of love.

Did she trust him?

"Tango 1 is down, confirmed. Joey, we're on our way. Hold tight."

Patrick shoved her toward the server access monitor. "Finish this. With just a few keystrokes, everything Zia Pharmaceuticals has worked for will be gone." He kept his gun trained on her. Joey looked back at Cole. Patrick swung his gun and pointed it at Cole instead. "I said, finish it, or Kensington gets another bullet! This one in his skull."

Joey flinched and put her hands on the keyboard. The program was almost finished processing. Ninety-five percent. Patrick walked toward Cole and pressed a foot to Cole's side. He cried out in agony, and her gut twisted in horror at his pain.

"It's still loading," she yelled through her tears. "Please stop!" Her eyes landed on Cole's and saw only anguish there.

He shook his head. "Don't," he whispered.

Ninety-six. The program marched another step toward its completion.

Joey pressed her eyes shut. If she didn't finish the processing for Patrick, then he was going to kill Cole.

And if she did, Cole would lose everything he worked for. It would destroy him.

"Come on, Alantara. It's just like old times. You and me, saving the world from corporate greed. Wreaking havoc on corrupt institutions and playing Robin Hood. The greater good, right?" Patrick's smile she'd once compared to a charming politician made her physically disgusted. How had she trusted this man?

She looked at Cole again, trying to send him a message with her eyes. Could he still hear the team? Did he know they were coming?

Ninety-eight percent. Her fingers itched, planning the keystrokes she needed to cancel the process.

"We're at the door. Breaching in three, two…"

The door to the server room crashed open. Patrick shouted behind her, and gunshots exploded in the tiny room like bombs in a warzone. Joey ignored the blast of pain in her ears and the urge to duck for cover. Forcing her fingers to skate across the keyboard to cancel the process.

Ninety-nine percent.

There were shouts behind her. "Get on the ground!"

The program prompted her to confirm the abort command, and she hit the keys hurriedly, a desperate prayer escaping her lips, hoping she wasn't too late.

The screen froze and she looked behind her. Cole was still slumped on the ground, his eyes closed. She looked back at the screen. There was nothing left to do here. Either she'd done it in time, or she hadn't.

Jackson and Ryder stood over Patrick, two guns pointed at his head, while Connor zip-tied his hands together.

She ran to Cole's side, cupping his face in her hands. His skin was clammy and his eyes glassy when he finally opened them to look at her. "You did it," he said through a weak smile.

"You know I'm right, Joey! You can't trust these animals. They only want your talent! We could do great things together, Alantara!"

"Anybody got some duct tape for his mouth?" Cole's raspy request made her laugh with relief and empathy. Cole was hurt badly. But he was still present.

"Shhh," she said, "just hang on. We're going to get you out of here, okay, love?"

His lip twitched. "Love?"

A tear fell from her cheek, landing on her fingers. She nodded and sniffed back the hot tears and runny nose.

"Come on, lovebirds. Let's get Kensington to a hospital."

"There's a helicopter on the roof," he offered with a wheeze. Joey perked up. Yes, a helicopter! Fast was good, especially with the amount of blood that seemed to be soaking through Cole's bright-white shirt.

"Is there a pilot?" Raven asked.

Cole shook his head with a wince. "I was hoping you had one of those."

As Raven directed the team and they helped Cole up, Joey stepped back to the computer to see what had happened with Patrick's apocalypse program she'd so desperately tried to stop. Her eyes widened at the message on the screen.

———

The ride to the hospital was torturous, every bump and jostle sending searing pain through his side. "All those movies where the hero chases a car or has a fight scene after being shot are completely full of it," he moaned.

Raven chuckled. "True. Anyone who's been shot can tell you that." His friend glanced back at him from the front seat. "Welcome to the club, I guess."

Cole groaned as they hit another pothole. Joey's hand found his with a comforting squeeze.

"Relax, Cole. You need to rest."

Cole knew she was right. The trip from server room to elevator to lobby doors had nearly done him in. The fatigue was harder to fight by the second. His eyes were heavy and the blissful, pain-free call of sleep dragged him under.

When he woke, he felt Joey's hand in his. There was a comforting pressure around his ribcage and a rather irritating beeping noise every so often, keeping him from slipping back into sleep this time.

He opened his eyes, found Joey asleep, hunched over the side of his bed, her head resting against his leg. He studied her features, though they were partially covered by her dark hair.

He shifted, trying to create more room for her. Ah, there it was. The pain cut through the fog of sleep and what he assumed were fairly strong pain meds.

Joey jolted upright. "Cole?"

He tried to say her name, but his voice was cracked and hoarse, nearly nonexistent.

Joey looked around, reaching out of his view and coming back with a cup of water. She bent the straw forward for him to sip, and he winced at the effort it took to lean forward even that little bit.

"What happened?" he whispered.

Joey squeezed his hand again. "They gave you three units of blood and rushed you into surgery. Other than the blood loss, they said you'll be okay. No major organ damage."

Cole felt a surge of relief. "I can't believe we got him. It's over," he said with a smile. "I love you so much, Joey."

She pulled her hand from his. "There's something you should know. I'm sorry. I'm so, so sorry, Cole." She put the cup away and then stood, backing away from his bed.

He frowned and reached for her. His arm weighed a hundred pounds and fell back to the bed. "What's wrong, Joey? Come back," he pleaded. Why was she leaving him?

Joey paced the room, obviously upset. He shifted his weight again, ignoring the sharp stab of pain as he sat up farther.

"Come here," he said through a wince. "Whatever it is, we'll face it together."

Joey turned to him from across the room, her brow furrowed and her hands clenched. She crossed the room in a few steps. When her hand rejoined his, he relaxed. As long as she was there, it was like his mind and his body were able to rest.

"Cole. In the server room… Patrick's program. I didn't realize what had happened."

Cole frowned, trying to follow her jumbled story. He shook his head. "I don't understand. I watched you cancel the program."

She hung her head. When she looked back up, there were tears in her eyes. Something was very wrong. "I didn't get there in time. I was so close, but it…"

Cole's heart dropped to his stomach. "What are you saying? It's gone? All the research?" Everything he'd worked for, the money and time he'd spent pouring into long shot drug therapies. All the work they'd done mapping the effect of genetics on different dementia conditions. Everything was lost.

What would he do now? When Patrick had his gun trained on Cole, he'd hoped Joey would save the data instead of worrying about him. What good was his life if his life's work had vanished? Then his eyes moved to their joined hands. Moisture gathered and flooded his own eyes in a moment.

All was lost. Yet somehow, he still had everything.

# CHAPTER TWENTY-SIX

COLE'S TEARS nearly broke her. She felt terrible. After everything they'd done, she'd failed at her mission. She'd been hired to protect the secrets of his company. And now, no secrets remained.

Joey shook her head. "No, they're not gone. Patrick wasn't trying to delete the server. I thought he was… but he uploaded it. Every confidential Zia file is completely public, accessible to anyone at the click of a button."

Cole tipped his head back, letting out a noise that quickly transformed to a wheezy cough and then a wince. She grabbed his water from the table and held it to his lips.

"Shhh, I know it's bad news, but you have to breathe."

Cole reached for her arm, taking a sip of water, and then meeting her eyes. Instead of the anger and despair she expected, Cole's eyes were bright and full of joy. A smile spread across his face as he laughed.

"So, it's not gone?"

She shook her head slowly. "Well, no. It's still there. It's just completely leaked. It made national news and everything," she explained. Maybe Cole wasn't understanding. Were his meds making him loopy? "All of your trade secrets and breakthrough drug research is out there for the world to see."

Cole was still laughing, a huge grin on his face.

"Cole! Stop it. You're freaking me out."

He paused his laughter long enough to say her name and lean back with a sigh. "I thought… You made it seem like it was gone forever." He shook his head. "And honestly, I still felt like the luckiest guy in the world because you were still here. *And I* was still here." He laughed again. "But then you tell me that it's not really gone."

"Yeah, but what about the company? Won't this hurt Zia's future?"

Cole's energy was fading. "Oh, probably. But you know what? I'd rather share every proprietary piece of information with the world than be set back a decade or more. Zia will be fine."

It wasn't what she expected, but her heart was full to overflowing with love and admiration for the man lying in the hospital bed in front of her. How easy it would be for him to be bitter about the attacks. Or, as she'd honestly expected, for him to blame her for not stopping it. But not Cole.

Cole's voice got quiet, slipping into the drowsy lilt of peaceful sleep. "Who knows? Maybe the next breakthrough will happen just because our information is in the hands of a curious graduate researcher at this very moment."

Cole's eyes closed gently, and Joey set his water aside, leaving her hands nested in his. Would this man ever stop surprising her? Or would her preconceived notions of what it meant to be Cole Kensington forever shape her expectations of the man.

It hardly seemed possible that less than two months ago, she'd been convinced that he was a member of the Syndicate and corrupted by greed and power. And now? She trusted him with her life.

Perhaps even scarier, she trusted him with her heart.

At the sound of a knock, she looked up to see Flint in the doorway. "Hey, boss," she said with a tired but contented voice.

"Hey. How is he?" Flint nodded toward Cole's sleeping form.

Joey patted his hand. "He's good. We're good. Everything is very, very good right now."

Flint smiled. "That's good," he said with a chuckle.

Joey laughed. "What about everything else?"

Flint came to the other side of Cole's bed and looked at his friend while he gave her the update. "There's a lot going on. Patrick is in custody. They already matched his gun to the shots fired at you in the alley." Flint turned his gaze back to hers. "We could really use you back at headquarters. Steven is doing great, but it's not the same. And Will and the team out there… Blue Smoke is a tricky mission, and the witness they're protecting? It's just… we could use you."

Joey nodded. Flint needed her. That was nothing new.

But Cole needed her, too.

"Maybe in a little while. I want to be here when he wakes up again."

The boundary felt awkward, like a pair of shoes she hadn't worn in a while and needed to break in. Flint simply nodded in response.

"I understand," he said. He got up and came

around the bed, stepping close to her. "When you're ready, okay?"

"Thanks, Flint," she said, looking up at him. "For everything."

He laid a hand on her shoulder, then leaned in to kiss her hairline. It was an intimate, fatherly gesture, and she relished the feeling of being valued and loved. Not just for what she could do, but because of who she was.

As Flint left, a nurse stepped through the door and whispered a greeting. "Let's see how your man is doing today, shall we?"

# EPILOGUE

WILL Gilbert stared across the bleak hotel room at Melanie Byers with a scowl on his face. The woman was terrified, that much was obvious. Of course, why wouldn't she be? She was the only witness to the assassination of the President of the United States.

It was just his luck that some innocent hotel clerk without two licks of sense would have stumbled into the assassination, winding up with a huge target on her back.

Which meant not only did he have to capture the man who killed President Walters, he had to keep that professional hitman from killing the woman sitting across from him on a dingy comforter. Her hair was falling out of its confines, framing her face with wispy strands. She stared at her hands, like she had been for the last ten minutes.

"Tell me again," he commanded.

She jerked at his voice, and Will felt a twinge of regret at his harsh tone.

"Sorry. I didn't mean to startle you." he tried again. "I'm just trying to piece together everything that happened."

Melanie's eyes were wide as she looked at him. Fear? Maybe. That didn't seem quite right though.

"Sure. I'll tell you whatever you want to know. I really appreciate you guys taking care of me."

Will grunted. As though they had much choice. When the man you were hunting was hunting someone else? It was in your best interest to know where they were.

———

Hannah Stone wanted nothing more than to lay back on the lumpy pillows of this two-bit motel and fall asleep for a month.

Well, maybe not nothing. The other thing she wanted was to pull her mini recorder out of her bag and demand answers from the commando sergeant holding her hostage. Who was he? What military branch did he work for?

So far, all her questions had been met with a complete stonewall. She knew his name–Will. And she knew that he had a surprising, yet charming southern accent. Other than that? Nada. Some reporter she was.

Which was absolutely not something she was going to share with G.I. Joe over there. As far as he knew, she worked at the hotel where the assassination happened. She was Melanie, according to the nametag she stole from the hotel breakroom.

Judging by his snarky comments about the press anytime the news came on, he wouldn't be happy to hear that she'd actually been a reporter trying to do whatever it took to get some exclusive material for her article about President Walters and the hurricane relief.

After this, she'd have the story of a lifetime. If Will didn't find out who she really was and decide that protecting her from the assassin was more hassle than it was worth.

# BONUS EPILOGUE

## *5 YEARS LATER*

COLE ADJUSTED the microphone and held up a hand to acknowledge the applause at the large press conference. Joey stood on stage with him, and though she was just behind his line of sight, he could feel the support of her presence.

"Thank you all. Thank you for coming today to celebrate with us a new era in Alzheimer's research. When our confidential data was accidentally released to the world, I remember thinking about how God might take that and use it to do something bigger than I ever dreamed."

He glanced back toward his wife and smiled warmly, thinking of that day in the hospital.

"What Patrick Wragge and his misguided accomplice meant as a blow to cripple our company and rob us from the opportunity to create lifesaving medicine has actually allowed Zia Pharmaceuticals, in newly established partnerships with talented researchers all over the globe, to make one of the greatest leaps forward in Alzheimer's prevention therapies."

It hadn't been obvious to him until a few years into this process, but there was no question that what others meant for evil, God had turned around for good. And if left to his own plans, Cole never would have made the decision to share everything. Bits and pieces perhaps, to established research partners. But never the entire catalogue of data.

"With our data made public five years ago, Dr. Vivian Fowler reached out and offered a potential solution based on her extensive research in a related field. Her suggested delivery vector was the key to an even greater improvement in the plaque barrier proteins than we had seen previously. Those incredible initial results have now been replicated by more than a dozen laboratories around the world."

He paused for the applause to subside. "Since that time, the Cognitive Protective Barrier therapy has requested and been approved for a fast track approval process from the FDA following the recent successful phase two clinical trials. We are moving into phase three trials, with optimistic—and educated—hope that the large-scale, long-term results are the breakthrough this community has been waiting for."

Cole couldn't disguise the pride and joy in his announcement. Everything he'd worked for was coming to fruition. And while there were still many years of work to be done, he knew the important thing wasn't that he'd finally reached his goal. Laying in that hospital bed, he'd realized that he knew the answer to Flint's question. If he worked all his life toward a cure and at the end of the day he only had Jesus? That was enough.

That he also had Joey by his side was a grace he hadn't expected. That he was spearheading a break-through preventative gene therapy to fight the disease that had devastated his family? An incredible blessing and honor.

But in order for both of those things to happen the way they had, he had been forced to rest in God's plan and trust Him.

"Furthermore, I am pleased to announce that CPB will be the first ever open-source gene protein ther-apy, the intellectual property for which will be one-hundred-percent available for any established biologic manufacturer to provide after they receive approval."

He turned to Joey again, waved her forward as the audience applauded. He wrapped his arm around her waist as he finished his speech.

"Once again, thank you to all who have followed our journey, prayed for our research, and donated to this cause. Because of you, we are on the brink of dramatically reducing the occurrence of Alzheimer's Disease. And to those who have already experienced the devastation of this disease, or are looking toward the oncoming years with anxiety, my heart breaks for you. But I encourage you to find solace, as I often have, in the hope we have for ultimate healing on the other side of heaven."

With that, Cole stepped back from the microphone and held up a hand to wave to the small crowd. He tightened his grip on Joey. He knew that without her by his side, none of this would have been possible.

While his Director of Research took his place at the podium and answered questions, Cole headed off stage with Joey under his arm.

Before her, he never would have had peace about letting God direct the path for his company or his life. But Joey's unrelenting passion for justice and good-ness in the face of evil and darkness inspired him to seek the same. She kept him humble, encouraged him when he doubted himself, and helped him find that elusive balance of striving too much and resting in the Lord. Her fight with the Syndicate was far from over, but the future was bright.

Once they were behind the temporary curtain, she tugged on his hand. He turned, willingly pulling her into a kiss.

Joey tipped her head up to him, her wide smile open and unreserved. "I'm so excited for you, Cole. You've worked so hard for this."

He kissed her again. "Thank you, love. I know I wouldn't be here without you. It wouldn't be the same if you hadn't been here with me the last five years." His throat tightened at the admission. How could he adequately explain how much he loved this woman? "I wouldn't be the same."

He held her face in his hand and she leaned into it. "Neither would I. I think I'd still be the *best by* any measure though."

He raised an eyebrow and fought back a smile at her teasing tone. Her own laughter sparked his own and he chuckled. "You are the best," he agreed.

"And don't you forget it," she quipped with a cheeky grin.

Cole smiled with a light-hearted certainty. No, he wouldn't forget. He was planning to remember the special moments God had given him for a very long time.

And hopefully, many others would have the opportunity to remember their own.

Black Tower Security Book 3 – Critical Witness, available for Pre-order now!

**A presidential assassin is on the loose, and she's the key to unlocking his identity.**

**But it's her own identity that is going to blow up the entire operation—and her future with the hero who saved her.**

# NOTE TO READERS

Thank you for picking up (or downloading!) this book. If you enjoyed it, please consider taking a minute to leave a review or rating. I hope you are looking forward to Will and Melanie's story as much as I am!

I'll admit, I'm a little sad to say good-bye to Joey and Cole. I loved their banter and their passion. But, I think they have a bright future ahead of keeping each other focused on the important things, while still changing the world for good.

I hope I've done justice to a story that touches the fringes of the Alzheimer's and dementia community. While I don't have a personal story to share, watching my friends struggle with the reality of this disease inspired many of my words and Cole's ambitions for his company.

While Cole's breakthrough gene therapy is based on similar therapies being tested currently, it was broadly a creation of my imagination. I'm sure I have made many mistakes when it comes to the terminology and technology used in the medical research community, but I pray the story rings true despite those errors.

If you'd like to play a part in supporting Alzheimer's Research, I recommend the Alzheimer's Foundation of America, which is highly rated and provides research grants as well as support for families and caregivers.

When we are face-to-face with the consequences of a broken world, just like Cole and Joey, we can place our hope in eternity, if we call on the name of Jesus as our savior.

I pray my books encourage you in your faith and through your struggles, whatever they may be. I love hearing the amazing ways God has used my words in the lives of my readers. It is incredibly humbling and encouraging! You can email me anytime at tara graceericson@gmail.com.

You can learn more about my upcoming projects at my website: www.taragraceericson.com or by signing up for my newsletter. Just for signing up, you'll get two free stories, including Clean Slate, the introduction to the Black Tower Security Series. It's the story of what happened with Flint Raven and Jessica before BTS was formed. Sign up to start reading it today.

If you've never read my other books, I'd love for you to read the Bloom Sisters Series. In those romances, you'll learn more about Poppy and Harrison Coulter, as well as Ross McClain, one of the founders of Black Tower Security!

Thank you again for all your support and encouragement.

# ACKNOWLEDGMENTS

Above all – Thank you, Lord. My only measure for my success is whether I have been obedient to your call. I offer these (and all my other) words as an offering to you.

To my content editor, Jessica from BH Writing Services. Grateful for our friendship, partnership, and how you make my stories better.

To Hannah Jo Abbott and Mandi Blake, for being the best accountability, prayer, and venting partners a girl could ask for.

And to the rest of our Author Circle -- Jess Mastorakos, Elizabeth Maddrey and K Leah. Iron sharpens iron. I'm so grateful for each of you.

To the Christian Mommy Writers, for being a place of light and community.

To Gabbi and Carla, for your unwavering support.

To my parents, for being a wonderful example of love, faith, and hard work. Especially to my mother, for being my extra set of eyes (and ears) for every story!

Thank you to all my readers, without whose support and encouragement, I would have given up a long time ago.

To all the other bloggers, bookstagrammers, and reviewers who read my books and share your thoughts. Thank you from the bottom of my heart.

And finally, to my husband. I simply adore you and our life together. I wouldn't be able to do this without you.

Mr. B – Sharing stories with you is quickly becoming one of my favorite things. Stay kind, sweet bo.

Little C – You've got me wrapped around your finger. I love to see you soar!

And Baby L – I'll never grow tired of snuggling you, or seeing your awe while you learn to navigate this world.

# CLEAN SLATE

## CLEAN SLATE

Read Clean Slate for free today by signing up for Tara's newsletter and find out how Black Tower Security came to be.

**She's running for her life. He can't lose her again.**

Personal trainer Jessica Street has stumbled into a money laundering scheme at her gym, and the people responsible aren't too happy about the extra liability. To make matters worse, the only person who can help her is the one man she never wants to see again.

Flint Raven regrets breaking Jessica's heart ten years ago when he chose his career over her. But the former security tech mogul isn't the man he used to be. When bullets start flying, he knows he'll do anything to protect her and prove he's worthy of a second chance.

Jessica has no choice to accept his help. But she's determined to protect her heart while Flint is protecting her life.

# CRITICAL WITNESS

Black Tower Security Book 3 – Critical Witness, available for Pre-order now!

**A presidential assassin is on the loose, and Hannah is the key to unlocking his identity.**
**But it's her own identity that is going to blow up the entire operation—and her future with the hero who saved her.**

Ex-special forces commando Will Gilbert is leading a black op tasked with bringing down the presidential assassin. When his team rescues a woman who witnessed the fatal shot, protecting her becomes just as important as finding their target and keeping the entire thing under wraps. Behind those scared eyes, this woman has the answers they need to finish the mission.

Struggling journalist Hannah Stone was in the wrong place at the wrong time. Or was it the right time? A Pulitzer is practically guaranteed if she can manage to escape without being killed. All she has to do is help Will and his team capture the shooter—without revealing her own identity as a reporter. Or just why she was at the hotel that day in the first place.

Pursuing the shooter and targeted by a powerful enemy, Will and Hannah face impossible odds. While her heart is quickly becoming tangled with his, Hannah hides her identity from the man trying desperately to save her.

# ABOUT THE AUTHOR

Tara Grace Ericson lives in Missouri with her husband and three sons. She studied engineering and worked as an engineer for many years before embracing her creative side to become a full-time author. Now, she spends her days chasing her boys and writing books when she can.

She loves cooking, crocheting, and reading books by the dozen. She loves a good "happily ever after" with an engaging love story. That's why Tara focuses on writing clean contemporary romance, with an emphasis on Christian faith and living. She wants to encourage her readers with stories of men and women who live out their faith in tough situations.

# BOOKS BY TARA GRACE ERICSON

**Free Stories**

Love and Chocolate

Clean Slate (Romantic Suspense)

**The Main Street Minden Series**

Falling on Main Street

Winter Wishes

Spring Fever

Summer to Remember

Kissing in the Kitchen: A Main Street Minden Novella

**The Bloom Sisters Series**

Hoping for Hawthorne - A Bloom Family Novella

A Date for Daisy

Poppy's Proposal

Lavender and Lace

Longing for Lily

Resisting Rose

Dancing with Dandelion

**Black Tower Security**

Potential Threat

Hostile Intent

**Second Chance Fire Station**

The One Who Got Away

Made in the USA
Columbia, SC
05 September 2025